CADRE KIDS

Cadre Kids

Larceny

Mary Mulligan

K&C Publishing LLC

CONTENTS

This book is dedicated
to every teenager that
feels alone, tormented
or afraid.

Know that your life has
value!

You will get through this.

PROLOGUE

Grand Union Flag

Freedom no longer existed, but they didn't lose freedom, they lost the illusion of freedom. The Grand Union flag, a flag with thirteen equal red and white stripes representing the colonies and England's Union Jack—instead of the fifty stars in blue—flew high above the school, the flag that flew in 1775 before America's freedom. Rosa knew it was a 'Cadre' signal.

Mike was the one that started calling the group 'Cadre.' He lived for Carpe Noctem, the nights when they all practiced Jiu Jitsu. The more the world became unhinged, the more Mike leaned on his friends. They were bonding closer than friends now. They were becoming family. Hard times and war tend to do that to people, so too can High School.

The clang of the hooks hit the pole rapidly in the wind. It sounded like a cracked bell being rung. No hymn, just clacking. Rosa stared up at it while her mind wandered to the Liberty Bell in Philadelphia, that summer when she and her brothers visited the historic cracked bell with her grandparents. It seemed like a lifetime ago. Back before the Cadre lost trust in her, back before she was compromised.

This was not their war and Rosa was mad that her friends sought to be a part of it. They were just kids, how much could they impact things? If she didn't have that one night, that horrible experience, she would swear they were all conspiracy nut jobs. The chill of the front moving in caused Rosa to shiver. The clangs like a cracked bell were more rapid now. Her brothers lived for history, war stories, and seeing relics like the Liberty Bell.

That massive bell rang for the first reading of the Declaration of Independence in 1776. Grandpa spewed on and on during that trip about the history of the tyrannical British government. She wished she had paid attention now. Ted and Jake did. They cared about history. That flag was symbolic. It represented something they were up to; it would be knowledge she could leverage. Baffled by their intent, Rosa regretted her exclusion as a Cadre. Inclusion as a Cadre ended the day after a 'Code of Conduct' was established. Jake thought of the idea in an effort to lure Piper into the group. The four of them already practiced Jiu Jitsu, but Piper had years of Muay Thai training. They all agreed she would be a valuable addition. Jake created it because a code the Cadres all adhered to sounded cool. He had no idea the strength it would extend solidifying their friendships to one another.

He also had no idea, how clearly it outlined that Rosa shouldn't be trusted to be one of them. They were originally all in this together, including Rosa, his twin sister. Mike was the one who verbally leveraged Jake's creation of the 'Code of Conduct' rules having Rosa removed as a Cadre. She was completely unaware that he did so all at Hunter's request. She couldn't blame Mike, she wronged him the most. No, she was angry, but she was angry with all of them.

She wasn't only angry at being excluded, she was angry that Ted and Jake went along with it favoring the others over her. They were her brothers. She was family. Family should always come first no matter the situation. For her brothers that apparently was no longer the case. That was one of the main reasons she did what she did. The group should have remained just the three of them with Nikki as lookout. Jake shouldn't have formed stupid 'Code of Conduct' rules. Ted should never have included Mike, and Mike certainly shouldn't be calling them the Cadres.

Rosa could try sowing seeds of discourse, but that would mean doing something against Mike. Mike at least tried to protect her once. It actually would be simpler to cause a rift between Hunter and Jake, but Hunter was the only one that didn't pressure her for answers. Rosa would have to be satisfied with being angry with all of them, but none of them individually. Dang it! She wanted to blame someone, perhaps she blames the Cadre that hung the flag.

Don't let someone else's darkness steal your light.

Rosa eventually looked up the saying after hearing it that dreadful evening. It turned out the source was an anonymous Pinterest post. Of course, how stereotypical of Abbey, a middle-aged mom. The saying made sense though and stuck with her. Absolutely no one was going to steal Rosa's light—not Jake, not Ted, not Nikki, not Mike, not Hunter and certainly not Piper. All six of her friends who formed the Cadre, but not her.

The Cadre was going to keep her at arm's length. It hurt to think about. Looking up, Rosa noticed brownish red stains adorned the grommets that ensured the flag didn't rip. Something must have gone wrong. Rosa swore she wouldn't be concerned. She was still angry with all of them. No, she wouldn't be concerned for any of them.

That brownish red color was the same as the color that covered her hands that night. Rosa subconsciously glanced down, as she often did since that evening, assuring herself that Abbey's blood wasn't there. No, it wasn't, and that was long past her now anyway. Still trying to convince herself, she thought she shouldn't be concerned over Cadre blood.

No one was concerned when everything Rosa worked tirelessly on for six months ended with a fatal mosquito swat. It was by design. Hunter, her enemy turned ally, was the only one who never pressured her for answers. None of them ever asked about her lost internship. She was trying to convince herself it was because they didn't care. It would be easier if they didn't care.

All Rosa wanted from that one stupid Philadelphia trip was to taste a famous cheese steak. Jake screwed that up. That was all she ever wanted, a simple taste of food. Food brought people together. Food helped people have something in common. Food mattered to everyone. That was what Grandma Mary taught her, FOOD FIXES EVERYTHING. No matter what, people had to eat.

Could food regain her standing as a Cadre? Maybe. Ted still gladly accepted the extra food she brought to him in secret.

Her thoughts wandered. At least she was able to see and stay with her grandma one last time that summer a lifetime ago. Her grandma, Mary, would spend hours with her, sharing experiences about being a chef in one of the fanciest kitchens in the upper East Side of New York City. She told so many stories, so many family tales—some true, some fables.

Rosa felt a special connection with Grandma Mary. It ignited her passion for cooking. Her favorite story was always of Grandma's mom, Rosa's great-grandma and how she only survived the Holocaust because she cooked so well. Grandma Mary often told it while making Poor Man's Cake, a recipe that didn't include eggs, because at the time very few people could afford eggs. Rosa noticed she put four tablespoons of cinnamon instead of the two teaspoons the recipe called for.

Poor Man's Cake

2 cups sugar
2 cups raisins
2 1/2 cups water
4 Tbsp. shortening (1/2 stick butter)
1 tsp. ground cloves
4 tsp. bitter cocoa
2 tsp - 4 Tbsp. cinnamon

Mix first 7 ingredients & boil 10 minutes.
Cool slightly and mix with flour etc.

3 cups flour
2 tsp. baking soda
1 tsp. salt

Bake at 40 minutes at 350 degrees.

Armed with her brother Ted's phone that summer, Rosa set the video to record as she took in the comforting aroma of that delicious cake being baked. She then asked the question she knew would get her the unabridged version of her favorite tale.

"I don't understand how that can be since, we aren't Jewish?"

Right on cue Grandma would explain how many Christians same as Jewish folks died, because Jesus teaches you to love one another and stand against evil. Targeting anyone with hatred is pure evil. Many non-Jewish people did stand up and act. Unfortunately, many weren't strong enough, they waited too long and most were killed as well.

Her solemn face and sad thoughts would quickly be washed away by pride. A smile would emerge revealing years of joyful wrinkles. She would then tell the story, a little different each time but always captivating.

"Great Grandma was one who stood up. When they came for her coworker, a fellow sous chef, Arnon, he asked her to warn his wife. And before you ask, yes, German women always worked. They didn't need some feminist movement to get them off their butts." Rosa rolled her eyes. She knew the feminist movement was important and their plight wasn't only about being permitted to work. Her grandmother smirked at her and proceeded grinning.

"Well, Great Grandma—doing as Arnon asked—ran straight to his house right in time to see Arnon's wife being taken away. The two made brief eye contact, and Arnon's wife gave her the slightest nod so as to indicate not to acknowledge she knew her. Your great-grandmother was distraught. Two of her closest friends were forcefully hauled away in front of her that day.

"Once all were gone, she sat staring at that house. The three of them all believed they would be safe if they continued to obey the law. They were only three people anyway. How much could they do? She knew deep down she failed her friends. Then the baby cried from inside. She ran in to find little Arnon junior hidden in the bottom of a closet. There was no way to reconnect little Arnon with mother or father. If she gave him to the authorities. Well, she had heard stories.

"Great Grandma took little Arnon to the church. The priest was livid with her. He pressured her to turn the baby in, pointing out it was too suspicious for a single woman to have a baby. The consequence to her, if that child started showing Jewish characteristics, was far too grave. Little Arnon already had a thick head of black hair. She refused, begging for help with any alternative option. The Priest then threatened to turn her in himself, if she didn't leave.

"Great Grandma knew God would not abandon her. She refused to do as the Priest demanded, disregarding any consequences that came her way. She sat crying for hours. The Priest finally came back with one of the nuns to help convince her to turn over the child. "Fortunately, the nun recognized your great-grandmother. The next thing you know, your great-grandma was working as an indentured servant here in New York, and little Arnon grew up as my father's brother Frank.

"Some say the moral of that story is that good people can always make a difference. Some say it is to trust in God, that He will never abandon you. I say, it is never underestimating the bargaining power of a delicious meal."

Rosa played that private video on the YouTube channel to herself every night while she sat in the Assistant Principal's assistant's office killing time. But like being a Cadre, her brothers and her friends had her access to the account changed, kicking her out.

Mad again, perhaps she should hope the brownish-red stains would be blood stains. A war was coming and Rosa had no choice but to be on the wrong side. She could only be angry about it—angry with her brothers, angry with her friends.

Yes, she would betray them again. She betrayed them because she loved them. All of them. No, if she was honest with herself, the last thing she wanted was for any of them to get hurt. That was how she ended up on the wrong side of this war to begin with.

Her betrayals didn't matter, they were only kids. What difference could a few kids make? No, they should be focused on surviving what was coming, not changing it. Her brothers, her friends, the 'Cadre' were on a mission and too stubborn to abandon it. Rosa couldn't help but reflect on what had brought her once happy extended family to a place where they were at war with the outside world, and to an extent, with each other—where some identified as Cadres— and she had lost the trust of those closest to her. As she continued deep in thought, Rosa realized that it all began with the day-trip to Philadelphia with her grandparents, ostensibly to see the Liberty Bell, but for her, primarily to get a famous Philly Cheese sandwich.

1

FOR THE LOVE OF RAINBOWS

Proclaim liberty throughout the land
unto all inhabitants thereof...

Rosa trudged along the sidewalk as if she were plowing through a blizzard, even though it was summer and the temperature was beyond stifling. Five minutes earlier, Rosa couldn't decide if the word sticky or stagnant described the air better that day, but now, having accepted a challenge from her twin brother, Jake, all she could think about was if she would be able to get away with it. But it was HOT and every step was leaden, requiring extra effort just to put one foot in front of the other.

Rosa was on a summer vacation outing, although in her family such outings included an educational component since she and her twin were homeschooled. It was late June, and as they do every summer, the twins were allowed to enjoy a month's vacation with their grandparents—their father's parents—in Catskill, New York. However, their Mom required a minimum of at least one day-trip involving a history lesson. Around the third week, they also stayed for a few days at their maternal grandma's apartment. Rosa viewed the history day-trip as penance for an otherwise great vacation.

This summer the history day-trip was in stinky, polluted Philadelphia— "Filthadelphia" as Grandpa called it—to see the Liberty Bell. Rosa couldn't believe this was the birthplace of America. In addition to the filth and heat, their grandparents picked the wrong Friday to visit the City of Brotherly Love—two days before the annual gay pride parade—and vendors, expecting informal festivities to begin early, were already setting up for a long weekend. It made finding a parking spot nearly impossible.

After parking what seemed like miles away, and finally arriving outside the building housing the Liberty Bell, then walking through exhibits in the Liberty Bell Center—Rosa found them boring—it was almost lunchtime and Rosa couldn't wait to eat. History bored the daylights out of her, but food was different. Everything food related she loved. Grandpa, meanwhile, allowed his excitement to build, considering the chance to see the great bell as their last hurrah of the day's adventure.

To alleviate a little of his own boredom, or maybe just because he could never stay out of mischief for very long, Jake dared Rosa to sneak a touch of the massive brownish copper bell. As she considered his challenge, she noticed that even if her fingers were sweaty. The bell barely had shine enough to reveal prints from her touch. It wasn't going to be easy. The bell was cordoned off by a metal cable to keep the public's grimy hands away from it—with the sole exception of people who are visually disabled—and Rosa wasn't at all sure she could reach far enough to touch it.

And there was always the factor of the guard, a hulking presence who looks friendly enough, and even cheerfully answers questions from the other members of the public who braved the summer heat to visit the bell. But there was no doubt that he was capable of stopping even the most determined rule breaker if the situation arose.

"Do it!" Jake mouthed behind Grandpa and Grandma's backs. "DO IT!"

Why does Jake always do things like this?

She noticed at least there was a slight breeze where they were standing and the breezeway offered shade. It seems so quiet, almost too quiet. No one was watching. Rosa knew why she was still sweating, and this time it wasn't from the relentless heat.

Can I touch the bell without anyone, especially that massive security guard, noticing? He must eat like a horse to be that size.

If she did it, the reward was Jake's promise to back her up on going to Caseus Magna's for lunch. Always thinking with her stomach, Rosa had researched all about 'good eats' in Philadelphia. Caseus Magna's was the spot for a famous Cheesesteak. It was a must do for any Foodie who was relevant in the cooking world. She was going to do everything possible to taste one. Caseus Magna's was conveniently located close to where they were visiting at Independence National Park.

Check on convenience.

That was a critical part in winning over their grandparents. Her hopes were completely reliant on Grandpa's arthritic knees, which would be flaring up by now, and a close place to sit would be a welcome reprieve. Caseus Magna's cheesesteaks were famous for using real rib-eye. Rosa could sense the texture of the cheese-drenched, soft, warm roll filling her mouth. Even the idea of the flavors made her drool. It was the time of year when the peppers were probably picked fresh. But if there were no seats, it might be a lost cause, because Grandpa would never agree to stand in Caseus Magna's long line to only end up having to eat as they walked back to the car. That was why Rosa tried to recruit Jake. She knew if she wasn't the only one asking, her chances of getting what she wanted were much better.

She hated asking Jake, her biological twin, for anything. Twin or not, they were nothing alike—even if all the people they knew referred to them both as "little Murphys." Murphy was their last name, and people used it as their nicknames. The famous 'we can barely tell them apart' usually followed. It was meant as a form of endearment, but Rosa knew better. Either that, or adults were really stupid and unoriginal.

Jake was a blonde boy. Rosa was a brunette girl. The adjective "little" was not just because they were preteens. She used to tower over Jake, but after a growth spurt he finally neared her height this year. Growth spurt aside, they were still both small for their age—maybe not significantly small but, still small. Jake would never sit still either.

How much more different can we be?

What irked her most about Jake was that anytime she asked for a favor, Jake wanted something in exchange. In today's case, the challenge was to touch the bell to gain his support for lunch at Caseus Magna's. He knew that touching the bell was against the rules.

Why can't he just be nice and say yes?

When not visiting their relatives, Rosa and Jake lived on or near military bases, following their father around the world as he pursued his military career. Currently, they lived near MacDill Air Force base in Tampa, Florida, which suddenly erupted in Rosa's thoughts as her gaze drifted across a potential ally who she hadn't considered—their older 'brother' Ted. Rosa realized she should have asked Ted. She just wasn't used to having him there. Ted was fourteen, two years older than they were.

How could I have overlooked him?

He was six feet tall and towered over her, Jake, and her grandparents. It was proof the heat was getting to her.

Ted wasn't a biological brother, but he was thought of as part of their family, nonetheless. Besides being much taller than everyone else, Ted was black, while the rest of the family was white, and while some may not have considered him an integral part of the family, the people who mattered did. Rosa liked Ted. He was perpetually happy and, unlike Jake he was nice to her. This was his first summer vacation with them.

Ted was Uncle Malcolm's son. Malcolm Cramer wasn't really their uncle but served as a Marine in the same unit as their dad. The two men had known each other longer than she and Jake had been alive. Both men often found themselves stationed at the same bases. Their current base was MacDill AFB, which was predominantly Air Force, except for some adjunct units much like theirs. However, their mom wasn't at all like Ted's mom. Their mother made it her mission to keep their family a tight knit unit. Platoon Murphy she called it. She homeschooled the two children at an intensity level that gained her the nickname GTM, short for German Tiger Mom. They called her 'the German General' when things weren't so lighthearted. At four feet, ten inches tall and only 105 pounds, she looked nothing like a general. However, you didn't want to be around if you made her mad. Homeschooling allowed them to easily move with their dad, and have a flexible schedule without the worry of disrupting school. Her goal was to keep Platoon Murphy as close as possible, specifically for their dad.

While Malcolm and Dad had been on several deployments together, something brought them especially close on their last deployment. Unfortunately, their mom wouldn't allow any conversations about it in front of the children, which only added to the mystery. Their mom even deemed it the 'No Go' conversation zone. After the two came home, Dad and Malcom were nearly inseparable. The children didn't remember a time when Malcolm wasn't called Uncle Malcolm. He often commented how he envied their family, and acknowledged he was closer to them as a family than to his own. Sadly, Malcolm and Ted only rarely saw each other—until six months ago.

Years earlier, Ted's mom claimed she couldn't handle the "not knowing" if her husband would ever return from war, and she separated from Malcolm when Ted was little. Ted lived with his mom in the Miami area, which logistically didn't make it too difficult to visit. However, his mom liked the attention of being a single parent and she wore it as a badge of honor, making certain Malcolm heard it repeatedly on every phone call and every visit with Ted. Visits became far less frequent as a result.

With no father figure in his life, problems arose as Ted entered his teen years. He often acted out, mimicking bad behavior he learned on TV, or from other children. Ted also started hanging out with the wrong kind of kids at school. His mom noticed instantly and got Ted involved in sports, which helped focus him on the right things, and gained him a new group of friends. As a result, he was excelling at school and hanging out with the right kind of children. However, the downside was it boosted his quirky new-found confidence, which only fueled Ted's disobedience towards his mother.

At home, his relationship with his mom could best be described as rotten. Ted made his mom's dating life hell. One night he crossed the line when one of her dates showed up wearing a 'pray for peace' shirt. Ted called the man a wuss, while he shoved him backwards out the door. That was the turning point. Ted's mom admitted she couldn't raise him alone and reached out to Malcolm. They decided that Ted should live permanently with his dad, and Ted's relationship with the Murphys blossomed. GTM welcomed the extra challenge of a third student, thus solidifying Ted in a quasi-big brother role to Jake and Rosa. Platoon Cramer-Murphy was officially formed.

Rosa thought about the start to that day, Grandpa was last to climb in the car.

In the coolest fashion possible he put on his reading glasses and said, "It's 106 miles to Chicago, we've got a full tank of gas, half a pack of cigarettes, it's dark, and we're wearing sunglasses. Hit it!"

Grandma looked over at him. "Kids, this is what Grandpa looks like after two cups of coffee. Be cautious speaking to him after one cup, and avoid him like the plague prior to that. And Hun, only us old people know quotes from the Blues Brothers."

While she really enjoyed having an older brother, Rosa was nonetheless a bit irked at Ted during the drive from the Catskills to Philadelphia.

Maybe that's the reason I forgot to ask him about Caseus Magna's. Ted seemed almost too excited to be seeing the Liberty Bell.

She made funny looks at him during the entire four-hour ride as he asked more and more annoying history questions. Grandpa was a slow driver, so even if the trip was around the corner his passengers prepared for an extra-long drive. Philadelphia from the Catskills should have only been around three-and-a-half hours, but with his driving, four was more likely. Grandpa insisted that the Liberty Bell was a must-see. Ted was starting to remind Rosa of Jake with all his endless dumb history questions. The ride was just painful.

According to Jake, vacation was the only reason for studying throughout the year. He knew the day trip history lessons during summer vacations were his mom's influence, but their grandpa always had a way of making them adventurous. Ted's being along added even more fun. Now boys outnumbered girls and, unlike Rosa, Ted seemed to enjoy history as much as Jake.

Grandpa rambled on: "In 1776, this bell was rung at the first reading of the Declaration of Independence—the reading was July eighth, not fourth. Actually, it is now rumored the bell may not have even rung on the eighth. Historians claim the state house steeple was under repair on that date. Although you have to be careful about people rewriting history. The truth becomes blurred. The bell cost America 100 pounds to buy originally from the English. The initial reason for procuring the bell had nothing to do with what it came to represent, or the English most likely would not have made it. Although big government is arrogant as hell, so who knows, maybe the dang Brits would have built it anyway. The bell was procured for Pennsylvania's new state house, which is now known as Independence Hall."[1]

Back in the Liberty Bell Center, Rosa was looking at everyone's back except Jake's. He was facing her, and now was rolling his eyes at her delay. She so wanted to taste the soft roll, perfectly cooked peppers, and cheese-smothered steak sandwich. Her stomach growled.

It's worth the risk.

Being small she was still an inch taller than Jake, so Rosa, staring at his arms, mentally measured Jake's reach. Hers should be the same. By stretching enough, Rosa figured she could cover the distance from the cable that protected the bell. If she touched down on her tiptoe with her right leg over the rail, extended her right hand, she could reach for a quick touch. Jake exaggerated his eyes in a nonverbal, "Do it."

Grandpa was about to move on, but paused when Jake suddenly quoted Frederick Douglass.

"I ask you ... to adopt the principles proclaimed by yourselves, your revolutionary fathers, and by the old bell in Independence Hall."

Ted never heard of Frederick Douglass. To stall further, Jake asked about the famous crack.

Crap, last chance.

Rosa was about to reach out when a minor disturbance caught her attention. A blind man had entered the room where the bell stood, and his companion, seeing the guard, asked if it would be permissible for her friend to touch the bell. Visually impaired people were the only exception to the touching rule. The guard instantly agreed, stepped forward and unclasped the cable and motioned the couple forward. With them in the way, the guard temporarily lost sight of Rosa and she seized that opportunity to step forward, keeping the new couple between her and the guard.

As the blind gentleman reached out to read the bell's inscription by touch, Rosa reached out as well. But as she stepped close enough to reach the bell, she instantly heard, "YOUNG LADY!" in a deep, booming voice. Sirens blared. The blind man jumped as if stung, stepped on his companion who screamed and fell backwards into the guard, who temporarily lost his balance. Rosa panicked, and tried to turn back, tripping and breaking her fall with her palms as she landed face first onto the tile. Ted, startled by the commotion, jumped backwards bumping into Grandpa, then fell square on top of him.

Grandpa gasped, barely breathing, "Ted, you are not light."

Jake howled with laughter.

The bellowing voice belonged to the security guard whose scowl was mean enough to scare the feathers off a hen. He appeared to be deciding what to do. He looked far taller than Ted and quadruple in girth. Even with Rosa's long brown hair pulled back out of the way of her eyes, her neck had to arch so much it hurt just to look all the way up to see the guard's face. Probably a good thing since she appeared to go pale once she got to his towering glare.

He is a giant! A mean scowling giant!

Grandma acted fast helping Rosa up, pretending Rosa injured her hands.

"Oh dear, we need to get you to a doctor," Grandma exclaimed, making an excuse to leave.

Quickly looking at Rosa's hands and turning them out of the guard's view, Grandma hustled everyone out of the Liberty Bell Center and away from Independence National Park.

In addition to just having Ted land on top of him, Grandpa had been on his feet too much that day already. Leaving the area at a fast pace caused him pain, which became a limp, thus slowing them all down.

These kids will be the death of me.

Finally, after moving a considerable distance away, Grandpa had to stop due to his aching knees. Jake was still howling with laughter, pausing only enough to say, "It was like dominos."

Grandma glared at Rosa and asked, "Why? And if you start with the name Jake, I will hand you back to that guard!"

(Silence)

"Hmm, no answer. I guess it's lunchtime anyway," Grandma said.

Ted apologized again to Grandpa, and commented about the massive size of the guard. Rosa didn't dare suggest Caseus Magna's— her misadventure convinced her—with no need for discussion, that Caseus Magna's would have to wait until another day as the group headed towards McDonald's, in the opposite direction of Caseus Magna's.

Jake's laughter was becoming contagious as he recreated the entire scene, graphically describing their stunned faces dramatizing their falls. There was no doubt as to why he won at the game of Charades. Not paying attention to their surroundings, Jake nearly bumped into a rainbow-haired, scowling protester, who appeared to be a man, but wearing women's clothing, who intentionally stepped in their path forcing the kids to sidestep. Taking advantage of the parade weekend ahead, many activists decided to protest for nongender bathroom usage.

Grandpa mumbled, "How far we have fallen."

This, or arms being crossed, was a sure sign Rosa and Jake could count on adding new swear words to their vocabulary. Grandma shot Gramps that look. As they walked on, it was Grandma's turn to ramble. "Don't listen to your Grandpa. She probably didn't see us. People in general are good. Both political sides just disagree on how to accomplish the same results. Who doesn't want clean air, safety or—"

Grandpa cut in, "Honey back in our day, there were centrists. The children don't have that luxury anymore, but you three are smart. Keep learning your history and you won't become a rainbow-haired freak show who isn't a 'she'."

"WHAT DID YOU SAY OLD MAN?" blared through a bullhorn from behind them.

Grandpa grabbed Jake and Ted, hissing urgently, "Get the women back to the car."

"I KNOW YOU'RE OLD, BUT EVEN YOU CAN HEAR ME THROUGH THIS BULLHORN. YOU DEAF OLD RACIST, CISGENDER, WHITE MAN!"

Ted snapped back, "Don't call him a racist."

Grandpa repeated, "Jake! Girls to the car. Girls to the car! Ted, he doesn't care that you're black. He just wants to pick a fight."

Jake and their grandma were pulling on Rosa, who was frozen scared, moving her down the street. They quickly vanished in the sidewalk crowd. Ted turned wanting the confrontation. The average person was normally intimidated by Ted's size until they saw his face and realized how young he was. The average person also doesn't have an angry mob backing them up, hoping for an excuse to target someone to focus all their anger on. Like most bullies, the bullhorn bearer saw the family in two ways, children and old people——perfect targets. The rest of the protesters not only started paying attention, they were heading straight for Grandpa and Ted from every direction. Grandpa saw the unfriendly crowd starting to form a circle with him and Ted inside.

He quickly grabbed Ted's arm, growled, "Now," and dragged him down a side alley.

The smell hit Ted like walking into a wall.

Port-O-Pottys baking all day in the Florida sun aren't this bad.

The rainbow-haired protester started jogging to catch them as best he could in ruby red heels and a yellow sequin mini-skirt. He held the bullhorn in his left hand, with his right hand balled in a fist. His bombastic voice echoed through the bullhorn.

"RUN HOMOPHOBE RUN!"

Hearing this, Ted stopped and squared off with the six-foot-five inch-tall-300-pound, mini-skirt wearing, rainbow-haired behemoth.

As the two locked eyes, the behemoth already had his fist in flight. But the protester had disregarded Grandpa, who hit the fist in flight, pushing it away from its target—Ted's face. The momentum and Grandpa's intervention also turned the protester away from them, exposing his back. Grandpa drove his knee into the back of the behemoth's right knee, which at the moment was bearing the bulk of his weight, taking him down to his level, which was at least half-a-foot shorter. Grandpa wrapped his left arm around the behemoth's neck, and threaded his right arm tight, which in less than ten seconds cut off the blood to his brain, as Grandpa simultaneously dragged him backward, preventing him from regaining his feet and his balance. The behemoth's bullhorn fell to his side as his wrist and whole body went limp. Grandpa gently lowered the behemoth to the ground.

"Give me your water, Ted."

Ted pulled the water bottle out of his backpack's side pocket without a second thought.

The crowd rounded the corner to see Grandpa leaning over the behemoth, pretending to be giving water and first aid.

Grandpa said loudly, "Please get an ambulance, the heat must have gotten to him."

At that instant four police officers rounded the corner. Grandpa kept up the act.

One protester shouted, "Wait, he did something. Arrest him!" Two officers pulled Grandpa aside. One said, "We saw what was going on. What did you do to him, old man?"

Grandpa whispered, "Choke hold. He swung at my fourteen-year-old grandson."

The accusers started getting louder and bolder. "Arrest him!"

The Sergeant on the scene turned to the crowd. "That's enough! We'll sort this out at the station."

He placed cuffs on both Ted and Grandpa as they were gently ushered into the back of a squad car. The behemoth was just starting to wake up when they were a good block away. The officer driving started smiling ear to ear. He then thanked Grandpa for the headache he just saved the police.

"Last week it took six police officers to reign in Cookie, after we received a disorderly conduct call!"

"That guy's name is Cookie?" Ted asked with obvious disbelief.

"Yes, that behemoth goes by the name Cookie," the officer responded. "The Peoplekind Coalition, which is the name they go by, already filed multiple lawsuits against the Philadelphia Police Department on Cookie's behalf, claiming excessive force against a woman, and more. Orders are, when it comes to Cookie, no matter what Cookie stirs up, we have to keep at an observation distance until something blatantly enforceable takes place. Old man, no offense but you against Cookie is a David and Goliath type pair-up. You were extremely lucky. We thought we were going to round that corner to see you dead.

"Anyway, the order to stand down is because the last thing the department needs was a repeat of last week, especially during Pride month. The reason we all now know and use Cookie's name is because, Cookie is 'gender fluid.' If we say 'he' or 'she' on a day Cookie is identifying as the opposite sex, another lawsuit gets filed. Apparently, my being the officer who used 'it' to address Cookie wasn't appreciated, and got my name listed on all the lawsuits' paperwork."

Ted piped up, "In school they tell us to use Ze. This way you don't have to worry about which one of the sixty-three genders a person identifies as."

Grandpa just sighed. The officer laughed and said to Ted, "From the looks of how Cookie is dressed today, technically you would have been beat up by a girl if it weren't for your grandfather. It's okay. My calling him an 'it' in the midst of battle last week most likely is the same reason the sergeant let me be the one to drive you two out of there. I'd rather be in the car. That heat is unbearable. The only thing worse was that stench. Five minutes more, and I would have had to burn this uniform."

He turned to Grandpa and asked, "Do you have a car parked nearby? And could stay out of the city for the remainder of the day?"

Grandpa gladly agreed. In a parting note, the officer mentioned to Ted, "The sensitivity training I was just forced to sit through now says there are eighty-four genders!"

Grandpa sighed, "Thank you, officer."

Grandpa and Ted got the car running and cool before the others arrived. Ted was about to speak when Grandpa said, "How dare you? You have a lot to learn! Not a word from you! That could have gone so much worse. What were you thinking? Why did you square off against a guy that was five inches taller and 100 pounds heavier? We were home free until you decided to challenge Cookie!"

Ted looked at Grandpa, confused, and said, "He didn't look that tough to me!"

When Grandpa spoke next it was with all the restraint he could muster, so as not to lose his composure. "Do you have any idea how close we were to getting pummeled by that mob? Did you for one moment think of anything but your ego? If I hadn't been there to step in you might be on your way to the hospital right now. How would I explain to the rest of the family that my grandson ended up in the hospital from a history day trip to the Liberty Bell?"

Ted spoke in the softest tone possible. "You called me your grandson?"

Grandpa looked at him, "Soldier's prayer—'Lord, let me not prove unworthy of my brothers.' My son Charlie, and your father, Malcolm, are more brothers than anyone else on Earth. That makes you my grandson whether you like it or not!"

Ted smiled bigger, "My grandpa is a bad ass!"

Faking the angriest voice he could at that moment, Grandpa responded, "Bad ass or not, you never put family intentionally in harm's way. Real men have something to lose. You walk away, or diffuse situations, even if you are one hundred percent in the right. If you absolutely have to fight, you hit first, and you hit hard. Not a word more!"

Grandma, Jake and Rosa climbed in, settling in for the four-hour ride. Rosa had been crying.

Grandma said, "See honey, I told you they would be okay. How did you boys get back to the car faster than us?"

Grandpa answered, "By the grace of God."

As they drove, Jake brought up Frederick Douglass to Ted again. "You really never heard of him? I thought you were getting A's at school?" Glad to share his wisdom Jake started, "Frederick Douglass was a famous intellect. In the early 1800s he was born a slave, fled to New York, maybe it was Massachusetts, anyway he worked on an Anti-Slavery Society or something. He was so influential, he is deemed 'the father of the civil rights movement.' During the Civil War he was responsible for recruiting the first black regiment to fight for the North."

Ted said, "I thought slaves didn't know how to read though? How could he be an intellect?"

Jake shrugged his shoulders and said, "He must have been able to read because he is really famous for advising Lincoln on the Emancipation Proclamation. He had like three Presidential appointments until Grover Cleveland removed him, but he even got appointed again after that."[2]

This was the first time Grandpa didn't help with a history conversation.

Jake waited until they were outside the city, distracting himself with thoughts of what it must have been like to be in the Civil War, but he finally sensed Grandpa's tension beginning to lift as traffic started easing up. With a chuckle he said, "Epic day! Rosa face-planted, and Rainbow Brite tried to attack us."

Rosa, feeling so relieved that they were all okay, was now trying hard to hold in her laughter. She muttered, "Great, now I am going to have nightmares about my doll." She had long forgotten Caseus Magna's.

Jake tried hard not to laugh louder, but he was finding it hard to breathe. As long as it was post second coffee, Grandpa rarely got upset. Now however was not the time to laugh.

Grandma pointed to a Baskin-Robbins. "Perhaps we should have ice cream to soothe our stomachs from missing lunch, and help hold us over until dinner."

Grandpa changed lanes, heading towards the ice cream shop. Looking in the rearview mirror at the three children, a dimple started to show in his cheek as he said, "Only if I can have rainbow sprinkles on mine."

The car exploded in laughter.

2

CHERRY FLAVORED CRUSH

D.C. Capital Building

"Pfff! Ultralight as if!"

"Hunter! Put my bag in the overhead and close it so no one else shoves their bag next to mine scratching it," said Megan, pointing with her long mauve painted fingernail.

"Why do you care Mom? It's always me they see carrying it anyway. Besides Porsche makes it, no way it will scratch. Now, if you buy the Guard Red 718 Boxter instead of this bag..." Hunter glanced back at his mother, but her eyes drifted to examining her manicure.

"Mom, you even listening?"

Great! Whatever.

All Hunter could see was her blonde hair covering her face while she looked downwards waiting on him. As usual he hustled into the window seat. No matter, she still moved at a snail's pace taking the aisle seat.

Why does she love making people wait?

Boarding first class, sitting up front ensured everyone passed them. Most all the men looked his mom over as they boarded. Why wouldn't they? She revealed so much skin her outfit was barely appropriate for the beach. Hunter locked eyes with one of the oglers glaring. "Perve," he whispered.

The man behind 'the Perve' looked away avoiding the situation. Megan's high heel 'accidentally' snagged his pant leg. Everyone had to notice Megan!

Picking up his iPad, Hunter inhaled a long deep breath.

If her perfume were ether at least I could pass out. Why does she act like this?

He squeezed his iPad until his hands turned red.

She's not an imbecile trophy wife. Her family's fortune makes the Harris name powerful.

One hundred percent true Italian heritage extended to Hunter through both parents, but fortunate for him, he resembled his mother's looks even her high cheekbones.

"Explain to me again why we are headed to DC?" Hunter asked.

Tilting her head, speaking in a higher than normal pitch, Megan answered, "Your father, the great Jonathan Harris, the most well-known Republican Congressman hailing all the way from Florida's prestigious district fourteen must attend sessions. Rain, snow, and even summer sunshine can't keep him away. You know all this!"

Pulling out the new, unstamped passport from his pocket, Hunter asked, "Tell me again why I got this?" Not anticipating an answer Hunter continued, "You know you initially said coliseums in Rome. Making me settle for 'in country' is supposed to be Martha's Vineyard, or the Hamptons—not DC!"

"We need quality family time with Dad."

Did she actually say that with a straight face? Does she honestly think this would rekindle their failing relationship?

Hunter shook his head.

(Bing!)

Clicking on the notification opened Facebook. There was a new picture posted of Mike with his mom, Abbey, standing on the deck of a cruise ship. They looked so happy.

"Why didn't you call Mrs. Swanson back? I could be with them right now on a seven-day Mediterranean Cruise."

He slapped her arm with the passport.

"Mike is my best friend!" Megan flicked her manicured nails in his direction and snapped, "They're new money."

Hunter didn't think things could get worse. "Oh, I hired a nanny, Maria. She barely speaks English. It was late notice so she is the only one available. DON'T run this one off!"

"SERIOUSLY MOM?" What a total waste of summer!

It was 9:00 a.m. that first Monday and Megan answered the door in tight yoga clothes prepared to greet the new driver the service was employing. In the past, the drivers assigned were former military so they could be tasked as security if the occasion called for it. Megan quickly tossed on a large blanketing t-shirt and pulled her hair back upon seeing Shabir.

"The drivers assigned to my son are supposed to be... trained?"

Shabir quickly answered, "Yes Mrs. Harris. I have former combat experience."

"But like US military? You are well, you know?" Awkward silence followed next.

Upon seeing this, Hunter shielded his eyes as he climbed down the formal staircase and walked out the front door.

Shabir added clarity with a grin, "I have combat experience working with the US military in Afghanistan, two years' time as an interpreter.

"Oh, um, here's the week's itinerary. Hey since you are an interpreter, maybe you can help Maria talk to Hunter in English."

Hunter was to spend the next three weeks on nine-to-five agendas visiting historic sites, parks and National Monuments with two strangers.

Mike is traveling the Mediterranean right now and I'm stuck being dragged to stupid historic sites by someone who doesn't know English while we are driven by an Afghan. Why is my mom doing this to me? Seriously. I'm thirteen. Why can't I just be left alone to play Fortnite. I could finally surpass Mike.

Hunter was busy walking to 'must see in DC' sites with a person who occasionally tapped his arm and pointed at things. On the third "'Mira" while Maria pointed, Hunter decided this had to stop. Although Maria not understanding English, posed one heck of a twist. More difficult or not, Hunter was still ending this.

What was her name? Maria?

"So what, it's another statue Consuela."

Wow this one is a special kind of stupid. Why does she even try?

When Hunter said sarcastic remarks at her all she would do was rub the cross around her neck mumbling. "Consuela that trinket isn't going to talk back."

Each place they visited was inundated with tourists. Hunter didn't know which politician said it, but whoever it was, was right about smelling the tourists in DC.

These people smell like the locker room after Friday football practice. They reek enough my eyes are watering. They aren't as bad as the occasional homeless person, but dang, they would benefit from a shower.

DC in summer was miserable.

Worse if they weren't overwhelmed by tourists, they were being inundated by morally righteous protesters. People were always angry about something.

Do they really believe gathering and marching accomplishes anything?

His dad called them 'useful idiots.'

I get the idiot part, but what possible use could these people have?

Normally Hunter could get a nanny to quit within a week. Not Maria, she showed up the following Monday morning escorted by Shabir for the second week. Hunter decided to double down on being cruel.

"Consuela you better have papers on hand or my dad will report you to Immigration and Customs Enforcement. You know ICE? Il ghiaccio." Hunter finished in Italian.

Anytime Maria tried to speak English, Hunter switched to Italian.

"My dad is going to revoke your citizenship status Consuela." Hunter said constantly walking away from Maria. He did so while crowds were at their thickest and took Uber home often without her consent. Shabir always rescued the day. He had been provided access to track Hunter's cell phone.

Megan's eyes were wide with amazement when she handed Maria a check Friday that second week.

Well this is a first. She must really need the money.

Megan fully anticipated Maria's return Monday morning for a third week.

Maybe not being able to speak English prevented Hunter from running her off.

Hunter gleamed as he overheard his mother that third Monday morning.

"I demand my money back! Your notification process is what's lacking." His mother's demeanor become rigid. "UNAVOIDABLE? The check already cleared. This was deliberate and yes, it is YOUR responsibility. As the coordinating service this is on you to staff. What do you mean there is no one else?"

Megan pointed into the air like she was poking a someone's forehead.

The person on the other end of the phone must have snickered because his mom went red.

"Did you just say late notice is an issue because word is out, I cancel checks on nannies that resign early."

Oh, this is getting good!

His mom had done that so many times before. To Megan, if a nanny didn't fulfill the full term of the contracted time, they didn't deserve payment for even a day of work.

"IT'S VIOLATION OF CONTRACT!"

The phone flew past Hunter's head.

Guess we will be going to the Apple store today. Why is she so hung up on leaving me unattended anyway?

Monday without a nanny began what Hunter described as 'hell week.' No, they never made it to an Apple store. Megan simply had a new phone same day express delivered. His mom constantly badgered him. She fixated on big things, little things, anything really that she could pretend to find fault with. She even found fault with his haircut.

There she goes again calling Dad. What's her complaint this time, I crunch too loud eating chips?

Hunter was starting to understand why his father worked ALL the time. Wishing his parents could get along made Hunter think of Sunday.

Can't they at least learn to text so I don't have to hear them bickering?

Smiling he Googled Roman Catholic Churches DC. The Basilica of the National Shrine of Immaculate Conception came up.

Wonder if it has a dome since it says Romanesque-Byzantine architecture. One of the top ten largest churches, Dad will like that.

Jonathan taught him going to church was all about being seen. Hunter didn't care, he just liked his parents being together and not arguing. But it wasn't Sunday, it was Wednesday. Funny his mom didn't complain yet.

Maybe Dad blocked her calls.

Hunter actually got away with playing Fortnite until 11:00 a.m. before his mom announced, "We are going to your father's office for lunch. Put on something better than THAT."

No way Dad is taking time to go to lunch.

In denial, Hunter still fancied up anyway.

No one ignores Megan!

Shabir opened the car door for them. He rolled his eyes for only Hunter to see, while Hunter's mom was saying, "Hunter don't get so excited. Your dad isn't anything special. After all there are 435 people in the Congress, same as him."

"Young men should be proud of their fathers," Shabir said. Megan slammed the door and raised the divider between the driver and passenger compartments.

Hunter leaned in, "Mom, he's the Chairman of the House Ways and Means Committee—the oldest committee in Congress and the chief taxing committee. It means something?"

"Did school teach you that?" She asked.

School? No one learns stuff like that at school.

"Don't you ever listen to him? Dad always jokes that he is entitled to any citizen's tax returns with or without probable cause, and no matter how above-board someone's taxes are, I can ensure they aren't."

Hunter could hear his dad's voice down the hall when they arrived.

"The Community Charter School Program bill is going to pass. The House Committee on Education and Workforce? They couldn't pass a sniff test from a hound dog. Look, the version we set forward WILL pass."

Oh boy! Here he goes again!

"America's school systems are failing. Measures have to be taken. The excuse of not voting to pass this bill is no longer acceptable. Twenty-five percent of children in America aren't learning to read," the Congressman added.

Wonder what poor sucker is on the phone.

"Illiteracy in America has a direct impact on other tax expenses. The quantitative figures show a fully literate society could start to make an impact in as quick as five years' time!" Newspapers, television, social media all were in first gear, bringing awareness to the Community Charter School Program. Lots of money was being spent to create conversation around the bill. Even bumper stickers were created: 'If You Think Education is Expensive, Try Ignorance!'; 'A Reader is a Leader'; 'Education is Our Passport to the Future—Malcolm X.'

Oh my gosh! It's never ending. Mom will shut this down. Let me aggravate her.

Hunter began rummaging through cabinets.

"CCSP is a Republican/Democrat bipartisan bill. It ensures a high standard of education. The school systems include focus on technical programs, allowing excelling students apprenticeship roles which will hold as much weight as university degrees. Kids will be able to bypass university and enter directly into the workforce. Parents will be provided vouchers to allow them to choose between schools. Everybody wins."

Irritated his mom hadn't ended this yet. Hunter discovered a large ornate globe which opened revealing a scotch bottle.

"Constraints on school choices include distance, and child testing scores. The scoring is done on a bell curve strategy. This promotes fairness and equality. The school is to be attended Monday through Friday, twenty-four hours a day, in boarding school fashion, five days a week. This eliminates costs associated with daily transportation. Blah, blah, blah... All children will benefit. I'm telling you this is the solution our country needs."

Hunter mimicked the one-sided conversation with his hand. Megan almost smiled.

"He's perfect," said Isabella, chairman Harris's aide, as she caressed Hunter's cheek with her hand. The woman was his height— tall, with dark brown almost black hair. Hunter never saw anyone like her. The slightest cleft in her chin made her stunning and unique.

Who are you?

Isabella was dressed smart in a white silk blouse with black slacks and black heels. Only the top button on the blouse was open to reveal a discreet emerald pendant necklace. It matched her gorgeous eyes that were gazing right at Hunter. Isabella was comparatively opposite Megan, his mother, in every way.

"Mrs. Harris delightful to meet you. Chairman Harris is in his office two doors down. My name is Isabella," she said extending her hand towards Hunter's mother.

"I know where my husband is," snapped Megan, ignoring Isabella's hand and pushing past her.

Isabella gracefully turned her unanswered handshake to Hunter. She embraced Hunter's hand softly and led him into a conference room.

Her hands are so delicate.

34

At that moment, Isabella could have led Hunter to the deepest pit in the earth.

Walking him over to a chair on the window-view side of the oval conference table, she asked, "Would you like a soda?"

Hunter nodded as a reply. Isabella walked a red Mountain Dew, Hunter's favorite, all the way over to him. While handing it to him, she bumped his knee ever so soft as she sat.

"Are you aware of the education bill your father is working on?" Hunter wasn't, but nodded yes anyway.

I'm nodding again, why didn't I just say yes.

"Would you like to help your father get it passed?" Before he could stop himself, Hunter nodded yes a third time.

What am I a bobble-head doll? How stupid I must look.

Isabella sensed his nervousness. To break the ice, "Can I have a taste your soda, I never tried the red flavor."

Wow! Her lips are touching the can where my lips touch.

"Call me Izzy. Isabella is way too formal for friends. Do you prefer pizza or Chinese food for lunch?"

Hunter was about to nod his head again.

I'm an idiot!

"PIZZA," he blurted.

"My preference, too, great choice."

She pulled over a three-sided flat conference phone, hit a button and dialed Avaroni's Pizza Rhea. She asked for three deep crusts, one Carnivore, one Berkeley Vegan, and one Roasted Garlic Chicken. "There, plenty to pick from."

Hunter stared at a waxy lip-gloss line tasting the flavor of cherry lips.

A woman like this works at my father's office?

Turning her seat, Izzy pointed out the window to the wide white marble steps.

"Tomorrow your father is going to speak at a podium at the center top of those steps. He wants to explain the Community Charter School Program bill to the public."

Hunter saw only her beautiful green eyes.

"Hunter, do you know there are 365 steps out there? Those steps are going to hold a lot of people. Do you know why there are 365 steps?" Hunter guessed, "For each day of the year?"

"Correct! Have you ever spoken in front of a crowd before?" The emerald pendant shimmered, but still didn't hold a candle to the dark green flecks in the eyes looking back at him.

"The Community Charter School Program is your father's way to ensure all children receive the best education. It would be much more powerful if you deliver the speech instead of your dad. You are the perfect example of a smart, well-educated young man. It's one thing to talk about something, but seeing the real deal, that's a much more powerful message. Those steps hold a big crowd, though. It will be very intimidating. What do you think? Will you do it?"

What a soft lavender fragrance.

Hunter nodded yes again. He hadn't even glanced out the window.

That afternoon Hunter didn't see his father or mother once. He hadn't noticed. Nothing could have been better than sitting next to Izzy prepping for his speech the following day. All he had to do was give a speech. He would go to the ends of the earth if Izzy asked. Izzy provided Hunter three note cards with bullets to practice:

Card 1:

Facts About Literacy in America

1 in 4 children in America grow up not learning how to read.

2/3 of children who cannot read proficiently by the end of the fourth grade will end up in jail or on welfare.

Over 70% of inmates cannot read above a fourth-grade level.

Card 2:

Nearly 85% of juveniles who stand trial are functionally illiterate.

Teenage girls who have poor literary skills are six times more likely to have children out of wedlock.

Reports show that low literacy rates directly cost the healthcare industry over 70 million dollars a year.[3]

Card 3:

This is direct evidence of the correlation between the ability to read and higher crime, higher healthcare costs, and more people on welfare. All of which cost taxpayers money. Pushing through the Community Charter School Program may be expensive, but it will save money in the long run. Children are worth the investment.

Around six that evening Izzy walked Hunter to the car service. Shabir was there to take him home.

"Your father will be wearing a blue and red striped tie with a dark blue suit tomorrow. Do you have anything similar? You and your father will be standing side by side."

Giving Hunter a reassuring kiss on the cheek, Izzy whispered, "Don't worry about public speaking. The most important thing to do is relax and be yourself."

That night Hunter practiced his speech dozens of times.

Maybe Izzy likes me. She can't be older than twenty-five. The note cards are simple, but if I nail the opening and closing statements Izzy has to be impressed. Perfect, this shirt is exactly what Izzy wants.

Hunter didn't know if his father even came home that evening. Megan rushed him straight out the door without breakfast. "Car service is here."

"Mom, his name is Shabir!"

Thank goodness it's Shabir. He always stocks soda for me.

Congressman Harris scheduled his press conference at 10:00 a.m., sharp.

"What's taking so long?" whined Hunter.

I hope I get to see Izzy before the speech.

"The drive was half this last night, what gives?"

Shabir had learned selective listening skills when it came to Hunter, but decided to reply. "I can't control the traffic."

Hunter Googled traffic accidents in DC. The search algorithms returned links with the top one being an article on DC being the second most congested city in the United States. Boston was first.

Stupid algorithms.

Finally arriving at 9:30, Hunter headed straight to his dad's office and heard his dad's voice bellow, "Megan did this on purpose!"

Hunter rounded the corner as soon as he heard him and entered his dad's office to see three people staring back at him. The scowl that came across his father's face hit him like a brick.

I made it on time, why is he mad? They still have a half-hour before the speech.

The older woman standing there laughed.

How dare she laugh at me. What a hag, she must be older than dirt.

Just when he was about to insult her out loud, she turned to his father.

"You had me going on this one, Jonathan. In all seriousness, I do hope you reconsider." She walked out of the room, shaking her head. His father didn't laugh at all, "ISABELLA."

"Hi, Hunter!" Izzy locked eyes greeting Hunter first with a big full smile, as she entered the room.

"Isabella, is this what you suggested Hunter wear, or is this my wife having fun at my expense?" Izzy, already knowing the time, pretended to look at a delicate silver watch anyway.

"Yes. I mentioned to match your blue and red tie. I can't imagine a shirt that does it any better. Was that Congresswoman Beagle threatening to kill this bill again?"

"Yes!" Jonathan rolled his eyes and pressed three fingers to his forehead.

What did I do wrong?

"Hunter your shirt looks perfect. Not many people can pull off wearing America's flag with such class. Do you have your note cards?" Izzy asked. He did, but the look on his father's face told him he should worry.

Entering the elevator Jonathan announced, "Change of plans. I will give this whole speech. If that shirt doesn't scream grandstanding, I don't know what does. He shouldn't even be at the podium. Have him stand off to the right of you, Isabella."

"Sir, Hunter has this speech down. At least allow him to stand next to you and read the bullet points. Grandstanding can't be inferred on pure facts. The emotional narrative of your speech will be hammered home when people see you as a father."

Congressman Harris shut his eyes took a deep breath and said, "Just read the note cards, but only when I put my arm around you. Don't say anything else, don't do anything else, and don't embarrass me worse."

Embarrass him worse?

Hunter transitioned to ant-man as they walked through the rotunda.

Embarrass him worse?

It didn't help that the rotunda was a massive room. The corridor leading to the doors was even grandiose.

Why was Dad embarrassed? He has to be proud of me, or why have me at the podium? CRAP, the crowd is gigantic. I'm totally going to puke!

The crowd spanned from one end of the vast stairway to the other. He couldn't even see how far back it went.

Super crap!

Hunter was staring at the crowd as his father stopped. Hunter bumped right into him. The glare protruding down back at him said everything.

Wow! Is he angry! Oh no, am I supposed to stand to the right or left of him?

Hunter's tan faded to paleness. He crossed his legs.

Why did I have soda? It's way too late to use the restroom now. Lavender?

Izzy's hand touched Hunter's shoulder. She whispered, "On your father's left."

I love you.

Hunter stepped to the left of his father, and smiled back at her.

She must like me too, to know exactly what I was thinking. I can do this.

As Hunter glanced over the crowd, a few people met his eyes.

They're all smiling back at me, no wait, they might all be laughing at me much like that hag. Why are so many people here for a simple speech? He looked at Izzy again. *She's not laughing at me. She's smiling at me. I got this!*

Chairman Jonathan Harris started, "The Community Charter School Program..."

The crowd was dressed in Sunday church attire mostly suits for the men.

They must be so hot.

Every few feet someone held a massive camera, usually balanced on a shoulder. Hunter glanced at all the different cameras. They looked like giant boomboxes thug-wanna-be rappers used to sport in old eighties videos. Hunter's shoulders relaxed. He swayed his head to the beat of the cameras moving in unison.

I've got this! How hard can it be? The only distracting thing is a group of people wearing prison stripes, holding signs. What on Earth is that about? Everyone should support education. What losers.

Minutes went by. Jonathan reached his arm around Hunter.

That is the sign.

Hunter rested the note cards on the podium.

Izzy said it is okay to read them if I have to.

Stepping in the center Hunter had to go on tiptoe for the microphone to pick up his voice. He started to read.

Remember slight pause between bullets to look out at the crowd.

He turned to Izzy behind him. He saw her smiling.

Don't forget glance at the crowd slowly, scanning left to middle to right, back to the card. Dang, stinking prison-stripe people. So totally annoying!

After completing the first note card, Hunter scanned the crowd before starting the second card. He stared at, and only at, the prison stripe-people.

Are they doing jumping jacks? Crap, I'm pausing too long.

Proceeding on to his third card, Hunter leaned forward towards the microphone the glass of water sitting there, spilled. It smudged out the words on the card. Jonathan Harris started to speak taking over as a rescue, but Hunter talked anyway.

"This bill will prevent illiteracy reducing crime, health-care costs, and welfare!" Hunter looked towards Izzy, who smiled and clapped softly. Jonathan Harris joked about how important this bill obviously is to Hunter and then conclude the speech. Then came questioning from the horde of reporters aimed at opposing the bill.

Why don't people like it?

The prison stripe people chanted, "Don't imprison our kids!" One reporter directed a question at Hunter, but his father refused to let Hunter answer.

Did Izzy see that, how embarrassing. I can handle a low-life reporter. Izzy trusts me.

As they stepped away from the podium another short, stocky man asked, "Hunter, how does it make you feel knowing if this goes through, you will only get to see your father on weekends?"

"Great! It would be more than I see him now."

Jonathan recovered with a statement, "Only because I have been working so hard on this bill. It is why Hunter is sacrificing his summer here with me, so we can spend as much quality time as possible together."

Hunter's smile extended from ear to ear. Izzy also smiled.

As the elevator doors closed Chairman Harris shouted, "You were supposed to read the note cards exactly. You sounded completely self-righteous, improvising that last card. How dare you talk over me! When I start speaking you stop! And how dare you answer that question. That reporter is a weasel. Never waste time validating his questions. Those people are not worthy of answers!"

Hunter went flush. His knees buckled. He grabbed the railing.

Why is he not proud of me?

"Isabella, take Hunter to get a soda or something. Just get him out of here."

Hunter was visibly shaking as they entered the little lounge area.

Izzy waited for Chairman Harris to be out of earshot.

"Forget your father. You did perfect! He's been doing this for over twenty years, and you were as great at that podium as he was today. You would have done better, I bet, if he let you do the whole speech like we originally planned. Hey, I had them stock up on red Mountain Dew. You want one?"

Hunter's trembling ceased.

Is Izzy telling the truth? Is Dad really envious?

Izzy popped the top on two cans and handed one to Hunter.

"I bet your father only lashed out due to that weasel reporter's question. Now he and your mother are actually going to have to be seen in public together, doing things other than going to church. His girlfriend isn't going to like that at all."

Wait, what? Did Izzy just say that? Dad has a girlfriend? How could he do that to me? All this time I knew my father avoided Mom, but he doesn't have to avoid me. Dad's choosing to spend time with some strange girl instead of me?

Hunter went to put the soda down, but there were stacks of bumper stickers everywhere.

"Something wrong with your soda?" Izzy asked. Hunter looked back at those green eyes.

She is beautiful.

"I didn't see any protesters doing jumping jacks with anti-soda signs."

He smiled.

Maybe he could forgive his father for wanting to spend time with the right girl.

"Since I only had soda so far today, I should wait to drink it."

Izzy's expression turned to shock.

"How did you not throw up? Public speaking is one of the scariest things a person can do. Polls show it is people's biggest fear. Speaking in front of even small groups is nerve wrecking. You just spoke in front of 300-plus people, your first time ever public speaking, and you did it on an empty stomach? Do you know how hard that is? No one should have been able to pull that off. That is like going to run a marathon and cutting one of your legs off the day before. Never ever do speeches on an empty stomach."

Izzy looked around and said, "Reporters will be crawling all over the Capital the rest of the day, so today is out. Want to do something fun with me tomorrow?"

Bobble-head-nodding-Hunter was back.

Did she just ask me on a date? It doesn't matter.

"Great!" Izzy jumped up, hugged him goodbye and said, "Let's meet here same time as today. Now, to tell your father I am taking tomorrow off. I have something very fun in mind. Hey, wear a hoodie if you have one."

3

OLD MAN BRIMMER

Shh. Listen. Do you smell that?
Dr. Ray Stantz, Ghostbusters

Platoon Cramer-Murphy spent the rest of the vacation far away from any city, at the home of their grandparents in Catskill, New York. Catskill is a Hudson River Valley town, famous for the story Rip Van Winkle, written by Washington Irving. Thomas Cole, the famous painter, often made it the subject of his oil paintings. Catskill hosted the Woodstock Music Festival and set the stage for the movie Dirty Dancing.

Sixty years ago, the Catskills, the large area of upstate New York, was the place to vacation before air travel became common. City dwellers loved that it was two hours north of Manhattan. Route 9W, better known as The Palisades Interstate Parkway, passes through it, as does Interstate 87. In 1984, Grandpa and Grandma Murphy moved to the Catskills excited to leave city life.

Platoon Cramer-Murphy didn't know any of this, or care. To them, the Catskills meant summer vacation. Each summer they fly to Newark, New Jersey—the smelliest place on earth—to be picked up by their grandpa and driven to their grandparents' home in the Catskills.

Rosa didn't need to look at the clock as they drove. It would only take about twenty minutes. "I can smell honeysuckle." Grandpa normally followed her observation, "Must be time to start looking for wild blackberry patches." He didn't have to look though Grandpa knew all the hidden spots.

The children filled many used Tupperware containers and sported purple mouths long before arriving.

"Why would your dad ever move away from here?" Ted asked.

In addition to living in an awesome location, their grandparents' neighbors, Mr. and Mrs. Sweet, had four children similar in age range to them. Although the Sweet children were mostly of English descent, their Scottish red hair made them easy to spot. Scarlett, nicknamed Scout for short, was the youngest at eleven, Max was the oldest at sixteen, Cody was twelve and Sam was fourteen. All were avid hunters. Even Scout knew the proper way to clean and prepare an animal. Her favorite was pheasant. Her father, Mr. Sweet, taught her that every time you kill an animal, make use of as much of the body as possible to honor it.

"How many new feathers did Scout add to her dream catcher?" Rosa asked.

"It covers the whole wall now. You will be in awe," Grandma answered.

Scout was so intimidating when we first met that Thanksgiving, until I found out she was just like me.

"Deer are too heavy for us," Scout proclaimed, hooking Rosa' arm and quickly leaving the boys behind. "I know deer hunting prevents deer starving during the winter, but it makes me cry. Promise not to tell?" That small secret bonded the girls.

The Sweets wouldn't live any other way. They often joked about not fitting into normal society. Normal society would deem them 'preppers,' because they could easily survive a few months without changing their lifestyle if disaster happened. In all honesty, they are just people who live within their means, don't believe in debt, and always are ready for a snowstorm.

Mrs. Sweet worked for the post office delivering mail, and Mr. Sweet worked for the New York Department of Environmental Conservation, assigned to the Rogers Island Wildlife Management Area as an Environmental Analyst. Neither occupation paid well, but they loved their jobs.

Mrs. Sweet often explained, "You can only be paid so much for the task of officially saying 'hi' to your neighbors on a daily basis." She loved gossiping and checking in on the townspeople. Mr. Sweet was the opposite of her, he could spend days observing nature and migration patterns barely speaking to folks. To the couple, living within your means equated to being frugal, but living their dream life.

It astonished them when they discovered a talk radio show by a guy called Dave Ramsey from Tennessee, who made millions teaching people the same thing.

"Debt is dumb, cash is king, and the paid-off home mortgage takes the place of a new BMW as a status symbol."

"Maybe not all southerners are bad. This Dave guy gets it." Mrs. Sweet said smiling as his show played in the background. "Be who you are, manage money well and retire with dignity."

He was even humble and joked about, "I don't teach anything new. This is something peoples' grandparents taught, but most of us were just too dumb to listen."

The other ongoing joke Mrs. Sweet told was, "We would long ago have been locked up for child neglect, because our children are what they call 'free range children'—allowed to travel unsupervised as far as their BMX dirt bikes can take them. Thank goodness I know everyone in town."

The Sweets believed assigning children responsibility and trusting them to be on their own, were the most important developmental actions parents can take. Children learn best from other children, and adults are for guidance and encouragement. Their children had three Cardinal rules. One, never ever go anywhere alone. Two, be home for dinner at five. And, three, pack a PB&J. They trusted their children to be smart. More importantly, they believed sheltering the children too close would cause worse long-term anxiety issues.

The oldest, Max, had just celebrated his sixteenth birthday that May. He was the first of the Sweet children to be allowed a cell phone. Treasuring it more than his driver's learner permit, he and Ted instantly bonded over technology. Ted had owned a cell phone as long as he could remember. Jake and Rosa, like the other children, had yet to be permitted phones.

Ted was ecstatic to teach someone two years older than he anything. "It is impossible to master all the intricacies and the capabilities since phones advance so fast, but I pretty much have it down pat."

Scout and Rosa kept in contact year-round via email. Scout had a unique way of being as skillful as the boys, but nonetheless an unabashed girl. Anything that wasn't a hand-me-down,

Scout would buy in bright pink or purple. Pink camouflage was made for her.

After that simple shared secret, the two were inseparable. Scout took Rosa under her wing even if she was a year younger. Rosa was initially nervous about being outside playing on their own. It was a relief to hang out with someone other than Jake. Rosa was always glad to hop on the 'girls are better than boys' train, since Scout was her first real friend.

The children spent the summers with their imaginations running wild. Each day they were outside—often before daybreak— fishing the Hudson, checking Have-A-Heart traps relocating nuisance critters, and pursuing endless adventures. Mr. Sweet always suggested the weirdest research tasks for them to help with, such as tagging Monarch butterflies or collecting moss samples. Jake's favorite game was playing Revolutionary War. The boys always made Rosa and Scout play the sympathetic Tories, so they could defeat them.

Often the children just explored the woods, or searched along the Hudson River on their BMX bikes. The Sweet children owned all four bikes, but since there were seven children, when the two families got together, they were willing to share. The children had pegs attached to the rear axle back wheel on each dirt bike. Although the pegs were installed for stunts, inventively one month a year those same pegs became secondary rider transportation. Scout and Rosa were designated passengers, being the smallest, while Max and Ted were designated peddlers, being the biggest, and Cody, Sam and Jake rotated turns.

"We totally can do it."

This summer Sam and Cody decided they wanted to become famous YouTubers.

"Max's phone has video. There's nothing else we need." Using an old gaming laptop, Sam was ready to setup their channel. "Now we need a focus theme."

"Why don't we make a car channel?" Max suggested, but was outnumbered in a one-to-six vote.

"What do you know about cars, Max? You've only had your driver's permit a few months and don't even have a driver's license," the other kids argued. Scout and Rosa both suggested a wildlife conservation theme. They were out voted five-to-three. Cody favored their idea.

Sitting around a campfire one evening, with a burning marshmallow at the end of his stick, Sam had a eureka moment. Mr. Sweet was teasing them all with the Brimmer Massacre story, claiming that they were the thirteenth-generation descendants.

Sam blurted out, "A ghost-hunting channel." All the children unanimously agreed to the plan.

Jake blurted out, "We could do Revolutionary War spirits." Mr. Sweet doubled down on scaring the boys, since he hated being interrupted.

He warned, "Whatever ghosts you hunt, always know Old Man Brimmer will be hunting you! It is why your mother and I prayed for a girl every time she was pregnant."

"See, girls are way better than boys," Scout triumphed with a big grin, as she held her head as high as possible.

Looking straight into his sons' eyes, Mr. Sweet looked around and whispered slowly, "Old Man Brimmer died a horrific death, trying to escape the violent pagans. It was the French and Indian War, which is even older than the Revolutionary War. The Brimmer family members were mere farmers, staying out of the war, but you can never stay out of war. You always must pick a side. War was all around the Brimmers. One day while Old Man Brimmer was making his three sons work his field, he came across a bright red Indian blanket, dropped intentionally by the murdering savages. When he leaned over to pick it up, an Indian swiftly galloped by, scalping him. He never even had a chance to yell to his sons. The Indians quickly killed his oldest son Jeremiah next. The other two sons, Godfrey and Jonathan, were still young. They tried to run, but couldn't escape."

Mr. Sweet paused while he ate his marshmallow. He looked around to make sure he had everyone's attention. The story captivated Cody to the point of burning his marshmallow.

"The longer a person's spirit lingers, the meaner they become. Worse, Old Man Brimmer was a mean man to begin with. Some say the two remaining sons, captured by those Indians, only survived the long treacherous march on foot to Canada and being sold into slavery, because it was better than living with Old Man Brimmer. His spirit is the meanest spirit haunting these parts. People file reports of an old man with blood oozing from his scalp all along these woods. It's Old Man Brimmer. He searches all the way from Bear Mountain up to Hoosick Falls. They don't realize he is dead.

"Ask your mother if you don't believe me. You don't think she pours salt on the porch lines every night to protect Scout and me, do you? It is a fact that every few generations, descendant boys of the Brimmer blood line go missing. You three boys are exactly the age that Old Man Brimmer hunts. That salt keeps him out at night. But if you're in the woods, how will you stay protected from him?" Jake wasn't going to be deterred by some fake ghost story. Sticking to the YouTube Ghost Hunter channel theme, Jake researched Revolutionary War battle sites, which are plentiful in and around the Catskills. One third of all the Revolutionary War battles took place in New York State.[4]

The children started at dusk the next day. "We will direct, since we own the phones," Max and Ted declared. The other five children rehearsed throughout the day. No one was left out.

All had specific assignments during the video. Scout's assignment was to shine the flashlight up towards the boys' faces for spooky appearance. Jake's assignment was to describe their location's history. Sam's assignment was to describe ghosts, pretending to be the expert on apparitions. Cody's assignment was to observe and spot sightings. Rosa was overjoyed that she was only assigned to pretend to add mysterious noises.

They all grouped up on their mountain bikes and went out after dinner that night. Except for two empty cars, the spot was completely vacant. The whole scene could have been out of any era in time, except for the cars. The area was dark and completely quiet—too quiet.

"Strange, you can't even hear a hum from crickets or locusts." Sam observed.

Jake hesitated as he looked around.

It's so scary here. It wasn't this spooky online.

"Maybe it's extra dark because of the cloud-cover hiding the moon," Jake said with a confident tone in this voice.

"You get an A for finding a creepy location Jake. This is scary as hell." Sam said.

Jake reassured them. "Hey there's a lot of us. No one is alone. We will be fine."

At least he didn't have Brimmer blood running through his veins. Jake glanced around to notice Sam and Cody fidgeting and breathing fast.

Sam came up with a save, mentioning that, "Video filming with phones at night won't turn out with good enough quality. We should come back tomorrow, do something different during the day."

Max nudged Ted and old the group, "We should try a test video." Pressing a button on his phone he said, "Look the quality is fine," Max fibbed. *Sam was right, it wasn't great.*

The two older boys planned to have fun. They were not about to let the younger boys back out. Seeing the nudge, Scout smiled to Rosa and started teasing, making flapping motions with her arms, calling them chickens. Rosa joined her. The two girls circled around laughing, flapping their arms, pretending to peck at the ground.

Cody blushed.

Rosa sees me as scared.

He still asked, "Does anyone else smell a skunk?" They agreed it smelled, but if a skunk was scared enough to spray it most likely vacated the area. Another excuse shot down. The teasing only became worse.

Sam suggested they start. "The sooner this is over, the sooner we can leave. Let's get this over and get out of here."

The three soon-to-be YouTube stars began.

Jake spoke first. Scout illuminated his face from underneath to give a shadow effect. Jake spent extra time endlessly explaining the history of the battle. He was beginning to have diarrhea of the mouth.

When my part is over, we will begin entering the woods. Let's not enter the woods. Keep talking.

Jake hesitated for the briefest moment. Scout turned the flashlight on Sam. Jake's turn, intended or not, was over.

The flashlight glowing on Sam not only indicated his turn, but that the boys should start walking into the woods. Instead of making a smooth transition, the three boys looked at each other, frozen. Rosa, out of video, already half in the woods, started flapping her arms. The boys knew they had to start walking or suffer horrific humiliation they wouldn't live down for years.

"Spirits like to observe from the shadows," Sam began. "To catch a glimpse of one, we are going to enter the woods." As the woods became thicker, so did Sam's words, "Most gh- gh- gh- ghosts, if we su- su- see any, are b-, be-, be- benevolent, harmless." His words then sped up, "They are friendly. They just are trapped in our world. They can't move onto the next world. They don't harm people. These ghosts are often seen by accident and mean no harm, no harm at all."

He hesitated. Rosa took it as a cue, and made the bushes rustle. Scout flashed the light around adding intrigue.

Cody didn't need to act. He was scared to death.

Old Man Brimmer wants to kill us. I am Old Man Brimmer's great-greatgreat-great-great-great-great-great-great-great-great-great-great-grandson. That makes me his number one target. I will be a goner for sure.

All three boys looked at each other. Ted and Max might not have been the biggest fans of the situation either, but they weren't about to show it. The more Sam's voice trembled, the scarier the situation became.

Sam explained how poltergeists are different from ghosts. "We will explore poltergeists in later videos." Telling himself, more than the camera, "Poltergeists tend to haunt structures. So, they wouldn't be out here in the woods. Poltergeists intend and will harm the living. They try to claim the structures they haunt."

Scout shined the flashlight around. As planned, Rosa knocked three times on a board. Sam glancing around said, "A Tommyknocker?"

Just as he did, two figures jumped out from the dark, "Booo!"

"It's the Brimmer boys, Godfrey and Jonathan," screamed Cody. Sam, Cody, and Jake, jumped on bikes leaving so fast they vanished like ghosts in thin air.

The two figures were barely twenty, wearing worn, ragged clothes. Not wanting to stop, they turned their attention to the remaining four children. One—who had funny ears—turned to Scout.

Without budging an inch, Scout shined the flashlight in his eyes, blinding him, and yelled at the top of her lungs, "GO AWAY!"

This did not deter the strangers. Funny Ears pretended to grab for Scout in zombie fashion. When his hand actually touched her shoulder, Scout let loose a blood-curdling scream of pure fear.

Rosa, the board still in her hands, jumped out from the woods and hit Funny Ears across the back. The man quickly reacted. Turning, he grabbed the end that hit him with his left hand, pivoting his body in a quick circle, grabbing the other end of the board right below Rosa's right hand, with his right hand. As he did, the force of the movement carried through the board to Rosa, sending her tumbling.

Catching Funny Ears off balance, as he hesitated after seeing Rosa fall, Max shoved him with all his might. Funny Ears landed flat on his butt, then rolled onto his back with his knees up and hands up. He looked like a dying cockroach. Ted stepped up to stand shoulder-to-shoulder with Max.

"She's a little girl," he yelled, still holding up his phone filming. The man's friend, who didn't get blinded by Scout's flashlight, was only a few feet away, holding his hands in a surrender position chest high. It was the oddest looking standoff. Both Scout and Rosa huddled behind Max and Ted, letting their brothers form a wall between them and the strangers.

"She hit me with a board!" spouted Funny Ears, as indignant as could be still lying on the ground.

Max chimed in, "I recognize you loser. Didn't you graduate years ago? Afraid to grow up and move out of Mommy's basement?" This made Funny Ears scowl.

Ted spoke, "Listen potheads, we have you on film toking it up. We took video of your faces, your cars, and your license plates. Now we have you on video pushing around little girls."

The other man, a few feet away, smiled at Ted. He still had both hands up in a surrender pose. "Calm down. No need for trouble. We will leave." He then lowered his right hand, to help his friend up, saying, "Josh, they are all kids. Let's go." He then apologized, "We weren't intending harm. We only wanted to have fun with a scare."

Turning his smile at Rosa, he said, "Josh's ex-girlfriends thank you for hitting him with a board. Do you kids want a ride home?" The children quickly declined.

Max, Ted, Scout, and Rosa's adrenaline spikes benefited from the long walk back. There was only one bicycle left behind, and all four couldn't fit on it.

Max's tone of voice changed to criticism. "Ted why did you back down? We totally could fight those guys. One even put his hands up already scared. You know they had to be stoned. What gives?"

Since they had plenty of time while they walked, Ted explained the lesson he learned on the Filthadelphia trip in full detail. This was the first that Rosa learned what really happened. Ted also learned from Rosa why she stupidly tried to touch the bell.

Ted then repeated his new Grandpa's line, "Real men have something to lose. Never fight unless you absolutely have to."

When they arrived back home, they leaned the fourth bike against the other three bikes perched against the picnic table. Sam, Cody, and Jake—having long been home—were busy planning the next video already.

Sam mustered up the courage to ask, "Hey! Max, can I have the phone? I have to forward the video. SSweet1776 is what we called the channel for Sam Sweet. The 1776 is because Revolutionary War ghosts will be our focus. After all it's the birth year of America. Cody found an image of the Declaration of Independence. We are going to use it as a backdrop. Isn't that cool?"

Jake added, "Yeah, we are also adding that William Jennings Bryan quote as the description, *'Our government conceived in freedom and purchased with blood can be preserved only by constant vigilance.'* The mention of blood will make it creepy."

Max handed over his phone to Sam. On any other occasion, he would headlock his brother for a stunt like this. The problem was all three deserved headlocks and he only had two arms. *How can I get even for them leaving us, running like Nancy girls?*

"Ted, show the footage of the two potheads?"

Ted had the footage playing immediately. "Aww, did Puff the Magic Dragon losers scare you? See? We have video proof your little sisters have more intestinal fortitude."

"Rosa hit him with a board!" Scout said, adding, "Told you girls are tougher than boys."

The boys appeared irritated. Remembering the girls' earlier teasing, Ted beat Max to their revenge.

Placing his hands on his hips, Ted did his best imitation of chicken, "puk, puk, pukaawwak."

Scout and Rosa roared in laughter, joining in, even hopping up and down on the picnic table. Max then cupped his hands over his mouth, and crowed like a rooster pretending to scratch at the ground. They were having so much fun being silly, pukaawwaking, and flapping to embarrass the three boys, they didn't even notice when the boys left and went inside.

4

BUMPER STICKER
BANDITS

Toasting a frosted strawberry pop-tart, Hunter texted
Shabir. He scribbled a note 'Gone to Dad's office.' He left the
townhouse before his mom saw him and his attire. He might
not own a hoodie, but wore dark jeans and a black t-shirt.
Arriving earlier than expected, Hunter sat at his father's ma-
hogany desk. No one was around.

A voice echoed through the hall. Hunter jumped up pushing the leather chair back under the desk. His dad was the second voice he heard. Perfume entered the room first.

Dang! Mom's perfume! Wait, is she giggling?

His father paused upon entering, but the giggle belonged to a busty blonde much younger than his mother. Her giggle halted and her smile disappeared when she saw Hunter.

This must be the girlfriend. Dad definitely has a type. I can't ruin my plans with Izzy. Izzy, the way she acted to Mom yesterday.

Hunter extended his hand, "Pleased to meet you. I'm Hunter."

Wow! I sound convincing.

The woman was carrying large coffees in each hand. Lipstick marks adorned both cups even the one with 'Jonathan' written on it.

Yup, definitely the girlfriend.

"Oh, excuse me. Let me put these down." She glanced at Jonathan who hadn't said a word yet. The glance communicated their mutual thoughts.

Did Hunter hear our conversation?

Eww!

Shaking her hand was like baiting a fishing line, pointy snags everywhere from the edges of her jewelry. Similar to Megan, she had long manicured fingernails and wore gaudy rings and clanking bracelets.

How can she sneeze in a tissue without scratching her face?

Despite this, Hunter kept smiling as the blonde introduced herself. "My name is Amanda." "Good morning Amanda. Dad, I know you are busy, I wanted to let you know I am here. Text me if you want anything, otherwise I will be with your aide today."

As he walked into the lounge, the bumper stickers caught Hunter's eye.

Mom would be furious if someone stuck one of these on her car.

He paused to read the slogans.

IF YOU THINK EDUCATION IS EXPENSIVE, TRY IGNORANCE!

Huh, catchy!

A READER IS A LEADER

Typical encouragement slogan—boring.

EDUCATION IS OUR PASSPORT TO THE FUTURE—MALCOLM X

Who's that guy?

Hunter's mouth hung open as he looked up to see Izzy standing there—dressed for a tennis match, sporting tiny white shorts, an American flag tank top, and Alpine Swiss red sneakers.

She definitely liked my flag shirt yesterday, or she wouldn't own one herself.

Izzy's dark hair flowed in a ponytail through a red baseball cap that matched the red of her sneakers. Without an ounce of fat showing, toned muscle gave her perfect curves with shoulder muscles well defined, and even the muscle above her knee formed a perfect teardrop. Izzy looked the picture of fitness.

Wow, is she beautiful!

"Follow me."

Anywhere!

"It's not an actual crime, it is more of a caper." Izzy said.

Hunter's eyes widened.

What the heck is a caper?

Before he had a chance to ask, Izzy elaborated, "A caper is kind of a prank just a little more deviant. How about the word antic? Haven't you ever been told I am sick of your antics? Capers or antics are the same things—sort of."

They were filling the black Under Armour backpack with all the bumper stickers that overflowed the tables where Izzy and Hunter last shared a soda. He will forever think of her when he drinks red Mountain Dew. There easily could have been five hundred or more bumper stickers.

"Capers are much more fun than pranks though, because there is always the possibility of someone taking it to heart. Therefore, the risk of actually getting in trouble does exist. So, the number one goal is not to get caught."

Fortunately for Hunter, Izzy came equipped with two hoodies.

Who knew lightweight hoodies even existed?

She handed him the solid dark blue hoodie, keeping the purple one for herself. It matched her personality, with her soft lavender scent.

Izzy suggested, "Let's wait to put them on. I made sure to bring ones with zippers so we can easily remove them if we have to hide. Hey! I even have matching handkerchiefs to cover our faces.

"Our first target is the parking garage of the Capitol. It is Friday 10:30ish a.m., so we should be able to sticker all the cars without running into anybody. Although since it is a Friday, the garage will only be half full. Avoid looking upward especially near corners so cameras won't catch our faces. Also avoid guards or people."

"Let's make this a competition. A CAPER COMPETITION! We can see who could stick bumper stickers on the most cars the fastest," Hunter suggested, smiling.

"Our challenge will start at the top floor of the garage, each taking opposite sides of the car rows, and descend as fast as possible to the bottom floor, OR as far as possible until spotted. Rules are we both stop and hide if we see anyone. If someone sees us, run to the steps and abandon the garage. If for any reason we get separated, let's meet at a place called L3 Bar and Grill on Pennsylvania Avenue. Get this L3 is short for Lawyers, Lobbyists, and Liquidity."

"Wow! Adults are stupid! Who brags about being a lawyer or, a lobbyist?" Hunter asked. Izzy chuckled at his thought process.

"Stupid or not, L3 is where we head. The loser of the CAPER CONTEST has to eat at least one chicken wing covered in the hot sauce of the winner's choice." Izzy left out the fact that the L3 Lounge has fifty different sauces some requiring waivers to be signed before eating.

"People can simply hire someone who cleans cars to remove the bumper stickers right? So, this isn't really doing anything wrong, right?" Hunter asked.

"Actually, bumper stickers can be removed with elbow grease and a straight razor, so people don't even have to hire someone. No, don't worry this isn't really doing anything wrong." Izzy reassured him.

My dad works here. Dad will really be embarrassed if I am caught. Wait, that Congresswoman Beagle woman works here. Wonder which car is hers?

Izzy noticing Hunter's hesitation said, "It will be fun. We won't get caught. Just remember to whistle if you see anyone."

They both took out about an inch-thick stack of bumper stickers. Hunter, displaying good manners, wore the backpack.

"Handkerchiefs up. I call the inside of the car rows." Izzy said.

Agreeing to go on the count of three, Izzy started counting, "One, two—wait who's that?"

Hunter turned, but it was a trick. Izzy was already on her second car bumper. The race was on. Heck it started without him. Slippery fingers prevented Hunter from progressing at as fast a pace as Izzy. He couldn't manage to get the sticker backs off quickly. Besides cheating, gaining a two-car lead, Izzy accelerated to a five-car lead in no time, finishing the first floor minutes before him. Upon turning a corner, Hunter saw Izzy's mistake in picking the inside row when he rounded the corner. Izzy had a ton more cars she had to sticker to keep her lead.

Izzy picked way wrong. She could easily be two floors ahead by now if she picked the outside row.

Hunter gained ground on her. For every car he stickered, Izzy had to sticker three. Not only did Hunter tie Izzy, he was now in front of her. About to turn to the next floor, Hunter heard.

(Beep-beep!)

It was the beep a car makes when a driver hits 'lock' or 'unlock' for the car doors. The beep came from a heavy-set man in a dark blue suit, with a yellow tie that drooped off his oversized belly. He was a disheveled mess. He wrinkled his suit jacket even more bunching it up over an arm, searching his brief case with the other hand. Hunter glanced toward Izzy. Izzy hadn't noticed the man at all.

Hunter was about to whistle to Izzy.

Wait whistling will alert the man same as it will alert Izzy. Worse, it will bring attention to us both. Wow, she is quick!

Izzy only had one more sticker to go before turning the corner, where she would run right into the fat man.

Izzy is too focused. It's a collision course in the making! I have to stop her!

Hunter stood up straight, pulled down his hood and hand-kerchief and walked on an interception path. Izzy ran square into Hunter. Placing a hand on each of Izzy's shoulders, Hunter gently turned Izzy in the opposite direction from the man. At three cars' distance away, Hunter looked back. The man was now putting on his suit jacket.

With Hunter's hands still on Izzy's shoulders, he whispered "Duck behind the silver SUV."

In silence, they watched the bumbling man. The man set his briefcase on the hood of the car still searching as if it was a bottomless pit.

This guy is taking forever.

Glasses! The man finally found his glasses.

He needs glasses. He probably didn't even see me and Izzy.

The two stayed crouched behind the SUV while the man waited for the elevator.

She doesn't mind my hands on her shoulders. Mmm lavender.

Izzy whispered, "I'm beating you."

In too loud of a rebellious challenging voice, Hunter said, "No you're not. I was ahead."

At the noise, the man, with his glasses on this time, turned. Izzy placed a finger to her lips shushing Hunter. They ducked lower.

(BING!)

The elevator doors opened, the man stepped in, the doors closed.

Hunter was quick to clarify the contest rules, "I am going much faster down my side than you."

Izzy argued, "But I hit twice as many cars."

Hunter, in fun, proclaimed, "Well, yeah, you have many more cars on your side. It's not my fault you picked wrong."

"New rules," Izzy proclaimed. "Whoever can get the most stickers on the most cars, between here and the stairwell wins. It doesn't matter which side you are on. Count out loud as you go. When we get to the stairwell, we leave."

Hunter pulled up his handkerchief and hood, "Okay, on the count of three."

Hunter went without even counting one.

I need every advantage possible. Dang she's fast.

By the time he was shouting five, Izzy was already shouting eight. There were only four more cars until the stairwell.

I'm going to lose to a girl. Thank gosh she can't tell anyone about this.

(BING!)

They both looked back towards the opposite corner at the elevator. The fat man looked back at them straightening his glasses. He saw the two sporting handkerchief masks with bumper stickers in hand. Between them was a row of newly stickered cars, including his car.

"HEY! STOP!"

Izzy and Hunter bolted to the stairwell. They hit the stairs on the third floor. Izzy was even faster at descending the steps than he. Completely out of breath when they reached the bottom floor, Hunter paused putting his hand on his heart.

"We can take a breather, the fat man is probably still waiting on the elevator." Izzy started laughing. She grabbed Hunter's hand, running, leading him buildings away and turned a corner before pausing.

"Let's hide the evidence," Izzy said as she shoved the hoodies, the handkerchiefs, and the remaining bumper stickers into the backpack before resuming their walk.

Hunter dramatized the walk by darting behind trees and slinking along the sidewalk as if he was an evil cartoon villain under surveillance. It made Izzy laugh. The more she laughed, the more he carried on. All their haste was for naught, since they arrived at the L3 Bar and Grill five minutes prior to opening at 11:00 a.m.

"Stop! My cheeks are starting to hurt even." Izzy declared.

Hunter, smiling back, announced, "I concede! You rule on bumper stickers."

I have never had never had so much fun. Please have mercy with the sauce heat level?

"Even if you pick the hottest level, that was worth it."

I wonder if the heat level she picks indicates how much she really likes me.

That thought was tossed out the window when Izzy selected one above 'her highest level,' and agreed to eat one with him.

"Have you ever watched 'First We Feast' the YouTube channel that airs 'Hot Ones'?" Izzy asked. "It's a show that interviews celebrities while testing the highest hot sauce level they can sample. If you ever learn to profile people, you'll learn an instant tell when the heat is getting too much is when the interviewee will slip up and curse. The only celebrity I wasn't able to call right on it so far is the famous chef Gordon Ramsey. Only because he says the F-bomb as consistently as normal people breathe."

Wow! Izzy's highest level is hot!

Seeing Izzy starting to sweat as she began drinking a second glass of water, Hunter suggested, "Here try orange juice. The sugar in orange juice mixed with the citric acid cuts pepper heat much faster than water. It tricks your tongue receptors."

"Impressive! I'm going to have to remember that." Over wings, Izzy treated Hunter as an equal. They decided to continue the caper and plotted to hit up K Street next.

"K Street is where people who think too much of themselves work. You know—lobbyist power players types. It isn't nicknamed, 'the epicenter of evil' for being Lollipop Land. We might not score a ton of cars to stick bumper stickers on, but the cars we hit should be considered high value targets (HVTs). "We have to be super careful not to get caught. K Street has heavy traffic, but the people are often so self-absorbed they will never notice us. We will have to work as a team, one of us acting as a spotter as the other stickers. We should keep an eye out for security guards, doormen, and even tourists. Basically, we watch for anyone who starts noticing or paying too much attention to us. If someone even remotely looks like they might be recording with a cell phone, we should abandon the caper. The actual goal, if uninterrupted, will be to slowly walk up the vast road in the direction of Georgetown University—AKA 'the Hilltop'—hitting every other car, the fancier the better. To better blend in with the crowd, we should forget wearing the hoods and handkerchiefs."

Hunter treated for lunch, but Izzy insisted on paying for the cab in cash.

"It is better for hiding our tracks."

She had the cab drop them around the corner from K Street. "If we head northwest on K Street, it should be a total of five city blocks before we should abandon and go to Georgetown."

Holy cow, pedestrians are everywhere.

Swiveling his head Hunter asked, "Does everyone walk around here? Cars are actually stopping at crosswalks. In Florida, people barely walk. It is just too hot. Besides, no one expects it. A person would be flattened doing this in Florida. Cars are actually stopping at like every intersection!"

Izzy started with a sticker on a Volcano Orange McLaren, with Hunter keeping watch. He then walked three cars up and hit an Indus Silver Metallic Range Rover. Izzy, encountering a scarcity of fancy cars, stickered a black Volkswagen. Two cars away was a four-door bright yellow Jeep, with a legacy Betsy

Ross flag tire cover. STICKERED! Hunter used the blue and white 'A Reader is A Leader' on this one, to match the colors in the flag. They decided to cross the road to be less conspicuous. Black BMW stickered! White Rolls Royce stickered! Red Mercedes stickered!

They stopped for a moment as they noticed a small crowd of what appeared to be reporters trying to nab an interview with a man in a black suit. No one even glanced at them walking by.

"Oh my gosh, look at those antennas!" Hunter exclaimed.

His next target was that news van. Izzy shook her head and reached for Hunter's hand to stop him.

A CMN news van Dad hates them. Those people make up stories out of practically anything. They embody the term FAKE NEWS.

Izzy missed! Hunter smiled at her, turned his back, and leaned in with his left shoulder down, facing the street and slapping a red Malcolm X quote bumper sticker on the van. No one looked. Izzy shook her head.

Not CMN!

Hunter wasn't watching. He peeled the second bumper sticker then the third. All three stickers decorated the CMN news truck. Izzy was pale.

"Hey! Hey!"

One of the cameramen yelled, as he pushed past Izzy toward Hunter. Hunter didn't turn in the slightest, as he jaywalked across the street. He knew Izzy would not be noticed. Heck, he was the one holding all the evidence in the backpack. The game plan was if they separated, meet at the "Georgetown Exorcist Steps."

Hunter wasn't in a rush though.

Izzy is bound to be impressed. I wonder if that weasel reporter Dad doesn't like works there?

Georgetown wasn't anything like Hunter imagined. Universities were supposed to be massive. This school at best was double the population of Plant High School, the school Hunter attended.

Maybe I can unload some stickers at the cafeteria.

Before even trying, Hunter discovered students on campus weren't allowed cars. Leaving a few stickers by the entrance, Hunter asked a student entering, "Are there bicycles to rent anywhere on campus?"

This was answered with a sneer, "All hills moron! The school is nicknamed the Hilltop for an obvious reason."

Okay, but why does that prevent using a bicycle? They should change that nickname from Hilltop to the Wimps. Haven't any of these losers been to San Francisco?

One girl was even complaining about the weight of the doors, as Hunter followed her into the building that housed the school store to buy a grey and blue T-shirt.

What does she expect with gorgeous old architecture? This school is small and snobby.

Hunter made a second pass by the stairs.

Odd...Izzy isn't here yet. She has my cell number, but I don't have hers.

He took an Uber back to the Capitol.

Crap! Izzy isn't here yet either.

He was about to leave to look for her, but his father, seeing him, pulled him into a conference room. The room was filled with people. Hunter sat at one of the last remaining seats at the table. He stared at the clock as they talked.

I am useless helping Izzy being stuck in here. Did someone catch her?

Hunter checked his phone. That kicked off notifications of messages.

('BING-BING-BING')

Crap when did these texts come in? Izzy was looking for me the entire time.

He quickly started typing, BACK AT DADS OFFI ...

Crap I am being asked a question.

SEND.

Pure silence filled the room as everyone stared at Hunter in anticipation of an answer. Someone repeated the question.

"Hunter, how did you know so many people cared about illiteracy?"

Is this woman stupid?

He looked at his father who nodded back.

Maybe this will get back to Izzy somehow.

Hunter stood and said, "When I realized most Americans couldn't even read at a fifth-grade level."

Claps were heard around the table, except from his father who only squinted at him.

Who are these people? Is Izzy okay? Hope she isn't worrying about me.

Hunter sat back down, focused only on the thought of Izzy.

At least if she is texting me, she isn't caught.

Twenty more minutes passed.

The conference room was almost completely cleared when Izzy burst in. All she saw was Hunter through the glass door. She hadn't realized Hunter's father and the lady who asked the stupid question were still in there.

"I see the apple doesn't fall far from the tree with this one," the woman said, nodding to Jonathan as she strolled past Izzy. Hunter just sat smiling at Izzy. He knew the Georgetown T-shirt he was wearing communicated to Izzy that he went looking for her. "Isabella, thank you for taking Hunter to visit my Alma Mater. You didn't need to take a vacation day for that. Heck my wife hires babysitters to watch Hunter, and here you do it for free."

HOW FREAKING EMBARRASSING!! Did Dad really just say that?

"Hunter what are your thoughts on the school?"

How do I change this conversation?

"The Colonial Architecture on campus is undoubtedly some of the best, especially Healy Hall. However, I may have to follow JJ to Harvard. Harvard ranks as one of the best schools to get an architecture degree. Cornell University, and Auburn University are also among my picks."

JJ, Jonathan Harris IV, was Hunter's older brother by nine years nicknamed JJ—short for Jonathan Junior. The two barely knew each other.

Maybe Izzy will think of me as old as JJ? They are probably the same age.

Jonathan Harris tilted his head as Hunter answered. Preferring the sound of his own voice, he started speaking before Izzy could even say a word.

"Isabella you weren't here for the feedback on yesterday's speech. Polling shows the people in this country are all talking about CCSP. A good portion of that is due to Hunter's involvement. We should have conclusive results Monday. You know this game, the more talk we can generate around education, the more top of mind it is to the voting public. The more top of mind it is to the voting public, the more we guarantee success. Perception is everything, Hunter, and no one likes being called on the carpet for not helping children. Hunter, please wait for me in my office? I would like to chat with Isabella for a moment. We can go to an early dinner after this. Phone Shabir?"

Did I hear him right? My speech was a success? Fridays are awesome!

After Hunter left, Jonathan turned to Isabella.

"What the hell were you doing with my son? Isabella, my wife has been calling me nonstop since 1:00 p. m., and you know how much I like talking to Megan. CMN aired footage of a boy identical to Hunter walking away from their news van, after vandalizing it with pro CCSP bumper stickers. Seriously, you had to hit K Street? Who vandalizes a white Rolls Royce with a red Malcolm X bumper sticker?"

The Chairman's veins popped out on his forehead.

Isabella smiled taking a step forward. Staring back at Chairman Harris she said, "Heck, I would have had him sticker 'The Beast' if I had access to it! Relax, the Director already confirmed the CMN video footage of Hunter is spiked. Now, I may play the part of your aide for appearance sake, but before you even think about getting red in the face when addressing me again, don't dare forget your role. This bill will be passed on Tuesday. Now, Chairman, do your job. Go back to Florida and get your home state on board."

With that Isabella walked out, grabbing the book bag and slinging it over her shoulder, smirking.

Hunter was the walking embodiment of conviction. Jonathan Harris approved of Hunter's insistence on helping out around the Congressman's office that last week in DC. Hunter called Shabir each day, priding himself on being able to avoid Megan in the mornings. The Community Charter School Program bill was passed as a recorded vote that Tuesday.

The entire news cycle the weekend prior was nonstop talk, not about the actual bill, but around the bill. Topics included low-level hit pieces.

'Blonde, racist, white boy wearing flag T-shirt calls America illiterate.' 'Jonathan Harris jailed—violates child labor law.' 'Bumper Sticker Bandits hit Senate Majority Whip's Bentley.' Hunter's favorite.

Chairman Harris was 100 percent correct. The more talk that is generated—the more top of mind education was to the voting public. The Congressmen who voted against the bill were the rare few that read it. The news isolated and targeted them. Even some Congressmen who read it, voted for it, knowing their voting base would never re-elect them if they were painted as anti-education. It was summertime—no one wanted serious conversation on the merits of an education bill. They wanted the latest Twitter challenge and lighthearted bumper sticker bandit banter.

The only downside to Hunter's week was that he didn't see Izzy in the office. Thursday morning, he forwarded her a link of 'the Bumper Sticker Bandit' article without writing anything. Most of the day had gone by, and Hunter feared he wouldn't see Izzy again before heading back to Florida.

She probably erased my number. It was that stupid 'babysitter' comment Dad made.

Sulking, Hunter went into the lounge area for a red Mountain Dew.

('BING!')

Clicking on the text notification pulled up a picture of Izzy in a red bikini sitting on the back of a sailboat with her gorgeous legs crossed next to a 'If You Think Education is Expensive, Try Ignorance!' bumper sticker.

5

FISH CAKE GALORE

That morning, after the epic 'ghost' video shoot, everything was back to normal.

Sam proclaimed, "I stayed up all night posting our first ever video. The editing software I tried out sucked, but at least it was free. Anyone know how to make a thumbnail? At least I think that's what they call it." He did so while rubbing his eyes. "Mom added a fourth Cardinal rule—videos are never to be switched from private to public until an adult reviews it. Originally, she said just her, but what if you guys make one? Anyway, she changed it to an adult."

Jake, Cody and, Sam having plenty of time the night before already collaborated on the next video which agreeably was a scary place, but scary during the daytime. The children found the place by chance while exploring along a trail of the Pal-isades. Collecting a moss sample for their dad, Cody lifted an oak tree root to discover a perfect hole, hollowed out directly under the tree. The hole went straight into the Palisades cliffs.

"It has to be a tunnel used during the Revolutionary War."

Jake researched back during the days when Washington's army —and the British as well—crossed the Hudson after the Battle of Long Island although nothing ever mentioned battle holes. The children decided that since they couldn't see the end of this tunnel, someone, on video, had to crawl to the back to see how far it goes.

Max blurted out, "We should film it at night."

"NOOOOO!" all the others shouted in unison.

"The tunnel must be man-made. Why else would it be a per-fect circle? It's only slightly bigger than a manhole cover."

They were all fascinated by it. The tunnel became their per-sonal, unsolved mystery.

"On video or not, that tunnel must be explored!" Sam said.

No one wanted to crawl in the tunnel. Besides being hidden under what Sam deemed a haunted, dying oak tree, the tunnel had dirt walls reinforced by cobblestone. "There is a real risk of it collapsing. Even if one of us is brave enough, eventually our parents will find out. After all, at least one adult has to review the video before we switch it to public. Whoever volunteers, involuntary or voluntary, is signing up to be punished."

"Mom and Dad never punish you as bad as they do us." This was normally what the boys said to guilt Scout. It held merit, which often persuaded her and worked in most cases. All those cases didn't involve snakes.

Scout's fear of snakes far overruled rational thinking. She wouldn't volunteer. She stood firm on not crawling in the tun-nel.

"I hate snakes! They slither, they swim, they are camouflaged, and they show up in awful unexpected places. Don't even get me started on how gross they become when they feed. No doubt a tunnel that deep in the woods, dug into the dirt, has snakes."

Since no one volunteered to crawl into the tunnel, the children decided the only fair way to determine the crawler, would be by the game of manhunt. Rosa joked it should be called 'People Hunt.' By either name, the loser had to crawl into the tunnel.

That night the children played manhunt as if their lives depended on it. If the tunnel caved, it might become true. Manhunt mixed the game hide and seek, with the game of tag. It could only be played outdoors, after dark. The more children involved, the better. The designated pursuer would count to a set number, while everyone ran off and hid within a set perimeter. After counting, the pursuer yells "READY OR NOT, HERE I COME," and has to search out people to find and tag. The main difference from hide and seek is if the pursuer sees you, and you can run away without getting tagged, you have the chance to hide again. If you get tagged, you are out. Tonight, the first person to be out would be the one crawling through the tunnel tomorrow.

The game allowed for multiple skill levels. This made it fair, since the children all varied in age and capabilities. An older, taller child may be bad at hiding, but a fast runner. Smaller children tend to be able to hide easier, but may not be fast runners yet. They could also just be good bluffers, yearning to sharpen their skills for future poker playing. Since most children know when the pursuer is onto their hiding spot, many will run early. A child in hiding could be super quiet, confusing pursuers into thinking they made a mistake, and get overlooked by staying hidden. The risk is the closer the pursuer gets to their hiding spot, the easier it is to tag them if spotted. It is all a game of figuring out how not to get spotted and tagged, in the creepy dark hours of the night.

"Ted you're our designated pursuer. You have immunity from entering the tunnel." Sam said.

"Is this because I'm the newest?" asked Ted. "I didn't think of that, but yeah that will make you the least biased on who you tag. It actually is your size. Even on hands and knees you'll barely fit in that hole," Sam answered.

"Hey big guys are often slow runners. You can't have immunity. If it hits curfew and you haven't tagged anyone yet, you have to crawl in the hole," Max added.

He then looked at Sam, "Ted's not that much bigger than me." No one said much at dinner, making the Sweet parents suspicious. In the neighboring house, the Murphy Grandparents were just as suspicious. The parents asked many questions, but the plan afoot remained a mystery.

Grandma Murphy caved. "This isn't the last meal and Testament, what gives?"

The children answered, "Nothing. We are just going to play manhunt tonight."

Grandpa blamed Grandma's cooking. "You should have grilled hotdogs. They're kids."

Grandma served Surstromming, a salted herring which is supposed to be caught right before spawning. It then is heavily salted to prevent rotting while it ferments. Upon hearing the explanation of her meal, Rosa stopped eating.

"No way I'm eating this!"

Ted licked his lips, "Delicious! My mom used to make me eat fish every night, I never realized I liked it so much."

Jake didn't care, "Can I layer potato chips on mine?" To this, Grandpa approved.

Rosa then asked, "Why couldn't they wait until after spawning? Why do they have to kill the poor fish while she is pregnant?"

Grandma answered, "It makes it much more of a delicacy this way."

What does that matter? Rosa scratched her head.

In the end, Grandma compromised, and Rosa didn't have to eat the fish, but did have to finish everything else on the plate.

"Your loss." Jake snatched the fermented herring off Rosa's plate, making a second fish potato chip layer. He called it, 'fish-cake tower' and ate every morsel.

The children all gathered at the picnic table out back. Only one person would be tagged, so the perimeter of manhunt extended to include parts of the woods behind them. Ted knew he ran fast so announced, "I'm doubling the time I count from fifty to a hundred Mississippi's."

The game began. Max ran off alone to the woods. He longed to become a Ranger sniper in the Army and planned use the game to challenge his recon skills.

Scout and Rosa decided to stick together. They were the slowest runners, and didn't know yet where to hide. They headed to the front yard of the Sweet house.

"Twenty-nine Mississippi!"

Sam, Cody, and Jake all ran in the direction of the Murphy house. The house itself had one of those wrap-around porches, which always made for a fun obstacle to hide under. The advantage being that a child could enter from either side of the house. Cody, being short, but fast, knew this gave him an advantage to outrun Ted, if Ted even found him. If Cody stayed with his back to the corner wall, he had a second advantage of darkness. Ted could look straight at him and in his cloak of darkness, still not Cody.

"Fifty Mississippi! Halfway there!" shouted Ted.

Jake—changing course—took off to the woodpile close to the edge of the woods on the side yard of the Murphy house. Grandpa had already fully stacked the woodpile by midsummer. It reached about five feet high. Instead of hiding behind it, Jake slipped between the multiple stacks for the best spot. Even if Ted circled the woodpile, Jake would be invisible. Ted would have to look in between multiple stacks, and shimmy through the stacks to tag him. This would give Jake time to shimmy out. He just had to be fast, because Ted had a seriously long reach.

"Eighty Mississippi!"

Sam broke off to the back left of the front of the Murphy house, which he second-guessed and changed direction. Short on time, Sam couldn't think of a good hiding spot, but quickly came up with a different plan. His new goal consisted of waiting in the center of the front of his parents' house, the Sweet house, until Ted called "Ready Or Not."

Ted was new to the game, so Sam hoped he would make the critical mistake of announcing which way he started going, by leaving in one direction while still making his announcement. This would allow Sam time to circle the house in the opposite direction. With Ted not able view the back of the house, Sam could head back towards the picnic table where Ted counted. Then he could hide behind the covered barbecue.

"Time! Ready or not, here I come!" shouted Ted, as he headed left towards the Sweet house.

Perfect! That is exactly what I anticipated.

Sam rounded the opposite corner of the front of the Murphy house, the furthest corner within the perimeter from the woodpile. As he circled the Blue Spruce tree, he literally ran into the girls who were crouched down, squatting on their knees behind it. Sam went flying. He landed on his elbow and rolled making a heck of a thud.

Crap. No way Ted didn't hear that.

Sam whispered, "Girls, are you okay?" Except for a mark from Sam's sneaker that ended up on Scout's bright purple shirt, the girls were fine. He got back up and continued with his plan.

Scout and Rosa panicked. If Sam found them, while not even looking for them, they had to find a better hiding spot. The two grabbed hands and headed for the porch. Ted lurked extra-long around the woodpile. After all Grandma cooked them that stinky fish dinner, Surstromming. Ted couldn't see Jake, but he smelled him hiding in the woodpile.

Jake's fish breath is so bad it can attract raccoons to the yard. He has to be near. Catching him will teach him to brush his teeth after dinner.

Ted decided to start squeezing between the stacks. As he got to the first intersection of stacks, his shirt snagged on a piece of wood. It caused a cascade effect in the opposite direction from the boys. This gave Ted an idea. He lobbed a smaller split log down one divide and heard nothing. He lobbed another down the other divide and heard a thump, with the sound of the slightest gasp.

Jake is there.

Ted needed to shimmy fast. As he did, logs were falling everywhere, but his determination to get to Jake prevailed. His size played a major disadvantage, Ted grew angry with himself.

Jake, on the other hand, took the wrong path.

Dang it, a dead end!

He slowly started to climb. Split logs were falling everywhere. Ted almost had a grasp on Jake, when the log that shouldn't have been disturbed, fell.

Both boys yelled. "Ahhh!"

The fallen log revealed a huge rat's nest. Momma rat, as large as a cat, sat straight up on her two hind legs hissing. Ted took down the other half of the woodpile getting out of there. By the time he did, Jake, more scared of rats than Ted, long vanished. Ted couldn't even see him running.

"Let's hide under the porch?" Scout suggested to Rosa. Hitting cobwebs with their faces, Rosa suggested, "Maybe we should hide ON the porch?" Hearing all the noise from the woodpile, Rosa added, "Ted's too far away to hear the creaking from the boards on the porch."

The two ran up top and gathered behind Grandma's and Grandpa's favorite wicker rockers. Grandma kept knitted Afghan blankets on both chairs. She always got cold, even in summer. The blankets hung over the backs of the rockers, down low enough that only the girls' feet were visible. The two were facing each other and smiling with pride from figuring out such a good spot.

Ted started looking towards the porch. His first choice would have been to hide underneath it. It's so obvious I bet someone is under there. He didn't want to crawl all the way under, so instead Ted looked under one of the entries.

It is too dark to see, and I can't hear a thing. The only way to know for certain is to crawl under there. Although I'm not stumbling across another rat's nest.

Ted walked clear around the porch towards the second entry.

The porch light has to provide better visibility from this side.

Seeing this, Cody bear-crawled over to the side Ted had just checked.

I can't believe Ted didn't notice the girls on top of the porch.

In the clear of getting caught, Cody found a chance to get even with Scout for teasing him in front of Rosa.

Cody took off his belt, slowly creeping it through the deck planks, ever so slightly rubbed it against Scout's bare ankle. Scout jumped sending the rocking chair over. Rosa unaware of

Ted, who was running up the steps on the other side of the porch, surfaced from hiding to check on what scared Scout. At that, Ted reached out and tagged her shoulder.

Scout's announcement of "Game over," could barely be heard.

It's my fault Ted tagged Rosa.

Ted repeated it in a booming voice, "GAME OVER!"

One after the other the children emerged from their hiding spots. Rosa looked at Scout, "Why did you jump out? Ted didn't see us."

Scout, looking back where she hid, said, "I thought a snake touched my ankle." However, nothing remained where Scout pointed. Just then Cody came out from under the porch, laughing.

Cody held up his belt and asked, "This snake?" Scout punched him in the arm, calling him a cheater, and yelled at him for getting Rosa tagged.

"Wait, Rosa got tagged? Scout, you should have been tagged, not Rosa." Cody's shoulders hung low as he frowned.

The children gathered back at the picnic table, making sure to yell "game over."

Now they could plan the tunnel search. Sam suggested, "We should use a long rope to judge the distance. It will help build the anticipation and suspense on video. We can tie it around Rosa's waist, and it would have dual purpose in case we have to pull her out."

"Pull me out?" Rosa looked to Scout.

At that moment, Ted noticed Max was still missing.

"Where's Max?" They all looked around.

"Game over. Safe to come out Max. Maaaaax? Maaaaax?" Suddenly the leaves and shrubs next to the picnic table moved. Max jumped up.

"BLAH!" They all jumped.

"You weren't hiding that close to me, were you?" Ted asked.

"Yup, the whole time, too. Don't worry, I won't tell them you picked your nose," Max said, gloating as he brushed leaves off himself through a mud-covered face.

"You really didn't hear me? I have been practicing during deer hunting season, but I hide before the deer are ever around."

Sam pretended to sniff the air around Max. "Max are you sure you used mud, not animal scat?" Sam then pinched his nose turning his head up in the opposite direction. Cody and Scout laughed, pinching their noses, also.

Ted pretended to defend his friend and put his arm around Max. "Don't worry Max. They are jealous of your recon skills. Besides Grandma served us Surstromming for dinner. Rosa and I can't smell anything over Jake's breath. You could be covered in poop from head to toe, and we wouldn't know."

Rosa didn't have even a hint of a smile. Scout's involvement prevented Rosa from telling her grandparents and having adults put a stop to exploring the stupid tunnel.

Ted then exaggerated sticking his finger up his nose. "Let's add boogers to the scat," pretending to wipe boogers on Max. This led to the typical "Say Uncle," wrestling match between the two boys.

Being ignored, Rosa stormed off and yelled, "Boys are idiots."

The boys looked at Scout. "What's her problem?"

Scout shrugged as she decided to hop on Ted's back in an effort to help overload him, letting Max win for once.

6

SUPERMAN HAS KRYPTONITE. JAKE HAS RAINBOWS.

Momma Rat

Gasping for air, Rosa opened her eyes. Pure darkness surrounded her. Something covering her from head to toe felt soft.

Dirt? It must be dirt.

She started to scream. A large warm hand clasped her arm, shaking it.

"Rosa, Rosa, it's okay, Rosa." Ted pulled the light blanket off Rosa's head. "Hey, it's just a nightmare." He clicked on the light.

It took a moment, Rosa calmed her breathing, and asked, "Ted what do you think it feels like to be buried alive?"

Ted nodded.

That explains the nightmare.

"Rosa, that old tunnel isn't going to cave in on you. Did you see those pavers supporting the inside walls when you get about two feet in? That tunnel is solid. Besides, I would never let you crawl in there if I thought there was even the slightest risk of it caving in."

Rosa clenched the sheets to her chest as if hugging a teddy bear.

Ted continued, "We are going to have a rope tied around you so you don't go too far. Any sign of trouble in the slightest and I will get to you before the weight of the dirt can crush you."

Eyes widened, Rosa whispered, "Dirt can crush me? I only thought it could suffocate me." Rosa tried to lie back down.

If only I can skip this one single day, vacation would be perfect. If I could wake up and it be tomorrow, instead of today, I would be visiting Grandma Mary, without those boys. Crawling into that tunnel would be over, a thing of the past, a total non-issue. I wish for tomorrow.

Barely touching her Captain Crunch cereal, Rosa sat silent, not talking to Jake or Ted.

"Rosa, I promise it will be okay." Ted whispered.

"Rosa do you know what a DEAD RINGER is?" Jake asked taking full advantage of the situation. With an evil grin, he continued, "Surely you must have heard of it, since it all started with food?"

Rosa looked at Jake, tilting her head back as if she smelled something bad.

Staring straight back into her eyes, he said, "It actually all began with old English porridge. You know, the stuff like the cold lumpy oatmeal Grandpa cooks us when Grandma isn't around."

Jake is making the situation worse on Rosa.

"Jake, stop. You're being mean," Ted said.

"You will be the modern-day version of a DEAD RINGER in the TOMB TUNNEL," Jake continued.

Rosa knew it was childish, but she stuck her fingers in her ears anyway.

I haven't thought of doing this since forever. Jake is winning.

Jake researched the saying, DEAD RINGER, the night before to discuss on the YouTube video. His breakfast audience was ideal to practice his new found craft of tale telling on.

Let's see if I can make this creepy enough to make Rosa cry.

Jake started, "A DEAD RINGER was developed by the English as a way to save corpses. England is a small country, so they began digging up old caskets from graves to make room for the new dead bodies. While removing bones out of the coffins, scratch marks were discovered on the inside covers of those coffins. People were BURIED ALIVE!"

"Jake, I said STOP!" Ted exclaimed.

Jake ignored him. "Since food was scarce, families would cook large pots of porridge for days on end in the colder weather. Pots of porridge sometimes would ferment if not stirred enough. The fermented porridge is blamed for killing some folks! DEAD! Or were they? Some weren't truly dead, though!"

Ted stood up saying louder, "ENOUGH JAKE!"

"Some of the stiffs were just passed out. In those days, dead bodies were buried quickly to avoid spreading disease. People were BURIED alive!" Jake paused.

This is sounding scarier than I expected.

Ted glared at Jake leaning closer to where Jake sat.

"The English began to tie strings to the wrists of corpses. That string would lead through the dirt up above ground to a bell. If a body was buried that wasn't truly dead, the bell would ring as that person gained consciousness. That person could then be dug up. So, a 'Dead Ringer' would be 'Saved by the Bell' from someone working 'The Graveyard Shift.' Three sayings we still use commonly today."

Jake glanced at Ted—breathing heavy ready to clobber him. *Here goes nothing!*

To put the last nail in the coffin—so to speak Jake said, "The rope Sam suggested we tie to you will make you, Rosa, a modern-day DEAD RINGER."

Rosa's eyes swelled as she slowly lowered her hands. Fingers in her ears didn't work. She heard EVERY word. Slowly shifting her eyes to Ted caused the welled-up water in them to let loose one solitary tear.

Ted lost it.

No one, not even Jake, is allowed to be this cruel to Rosa.

Cereal bowls went flying, Jake plead UNCLE before the minute ended. Pleading 'uncle' didn't cut it this time.

"Rosa, make Jake smell your feet until he apologizes."

Rosa started smiling as she stuck her rainbow-colored sock in Jake's face.

Grandpa turned the corner for his second cup of coffee. The children froze. It was a sight! Ted tangled around Jake like an octopus. His left arm held Jake's head still. His long right arm wrapped around Jake's body, pinning both Jake's arms down by his side. The chair was knocked on its side. Milk and cereal covered the table, the floor, the front of Jake. Rosa balanced on her left foot, with her right foot smooshing Jake's nose.

Grandpa paused, then continued to walk over and pour his coffee.

The children held the pose as still as possible all pondering the same thing.

How much trouble are we in?

Grandpa turned around, took a long taste of his steaming coffee, and stared at the three children. In an under-his-breath growl, he said, "Clean it up, and I won't tell your grandma."

Jake mumbled, "Yes, Sir," as best he could through the stinky rainbow sock.

"The woodpile too!" growled Grandpa. Taking one last look at the scene of the frozen children, Grandpa said, "Jake, Superman has kryptonite. You have rainbows." Grandpa headed back out to his newspaper and rocking chair on the porch.

It was afternoon by the time all the children arrived at the tunnel. Sam, anxious to create the second video, convinced everyone to chip in on helping clean up the decimated woodpile from the night before. Even though all were helping, the children moved slowly. Not a one of them wanted to encounter Momma Rat again.

Like the first video, they all planned ahead and scripted the roles they would play. Max and Ted were responsible for recording the video. Rosa was the only one pale and fidgeting.

Cody began, "During the Revolutionary War the British soldiers were much more prepared for battle than the Americans. Americans weren't professional, paid soldiers. They were farmers, blacksmiths and tradesmen, but they had better motivation. They were fighting for their freedom. The British expected Americans to stand up and fight in battle lines like paid professional soldiers did. Americans quickly discovered, that to survive, they must fight differently. One can say America's Revolutionary soldiers were the first to fight employing guerrilla warfare tactics."

Sam took over speaking, "British General, General Cornwallis, successfully led his troops into battle against the Americans, and was able to make the Americans retreat. Even though the Americans retreated, they retreated up Huyler's Landing Trail. This, Cornwallis didn't plan for. Huyler's Landing Trail is part of the cliffs down by the Fort Lee area. Cornwallis tried, but couldn't successfully follow. This empowered the American soldiers. Because Cornwallis couldn't follow them in the rough terrain, the soldiers used these cliffs as a safe haven. We believe this tunnel—"

Jake interrupted, "the TOMB tunnel!"

Sam continued, "—the tomb tunnel was created back during the Revolutionary War by some American soldiers."

Scout spoke next while she tied the yellow rope to Rosa's waist. "To our knowledge, no one has ever explored the tunnel."

"Tomb tunnel," Jake mouthed at her.

Scout continued, "We have searched records in the library regarding this and other tunnels in the area, to no avail. This is a fifty-foot rope. My best friend Rosa is going to crawl into the tunnel—" "TOMB TUNNEL," blurted out Jake again. "—either to the end of the tunnel or the end of this rope. We aren't sure what she will find. This flashlight will help her see what to avoid—like snakes."

They both looked at each other with anticipation and hugged.

Rosa avoided looking towards Jake's gleaming face. She glanced at Max who asked, "Any last words?"

"Sorry Mom."

That may be the very last thing I ever say to my mom. Maybe Mom will disown Jake if I don't return.

Rosa squatted down, hesitating to go to her knees and begin to crawl. Jake couldn't wait to start on his 'dead ringer' explanation again. He had it down pat after practicing it at breakfast.

The sound of Jake's voice made Rosa crawl forward. She slowed about ten-feet inside the tunnel where the darkness had become overwhelming.

I'm still close enough to the entrance Ted can pull me out if it caves. Whoever imagined dirt could weigh enough to crush a person.

For the first time Rosa tried the flashlight.

What a total piece of junk.

She recognized it too.

Dad gave this to Mr. Sweet as a silly retro gift last year. It went along with the standard old person term 'remember when.' Apparently, flashlights sucked in the old days.

She hit it harder to get it working.

Most likely Jake picked the flashlight on purpose. Finally, a soft warm glow came from it that barely provided visibility around her. Even in the weak glow, the flashlight revealed cobblestones on the walls and ceiling.

Ted is right.

To the touch, those stones felt solid and sturdy. Touching a few more helped Rosa lose all fear of a cave in and suffocation. Heck, even if the flashlight went out, she could feel her way along the stones back to the entrance.

How scary it must be to be blind? Now all I have to worry about are snakes, rats, and skeletons. All of which are scary, but none of which can actually hurt me. I can do this. After all, I'm the girl who hit a pothead with a board.

"Be brave! Okay, time to crawl on," Rosa said out loud to herself.

This has to be the crappiest flashlight known to man! Crawling with a flashlight isn't easy.

It flickered with every move of her hand.

If I move fast instead of slow, this will soon be over.

Something behind her made a noise, but the flashlight glow wasn't strong enough to see anything.

Maybe it's my imagination.

In front of her, something scurried.

What evil things could live in here? A Sasquatch? No way! A Sasquatch would never fit in this tunnel. Ted couldn't even fit in this tunnel. Wonder if Sasquatches are really bad or just misunderstood big hairy giants.

The flashlight flickered out.

Dang flashlight! Wonder how far of a distance we peddled. Could we have made it far enough to be in New Jersey? If the myth of the Jersey Devil is real, could that have been him? Wait, didn't that myth have the creature living in south Jersey in the Pine Barrens? Then again, it is a devil. Can't a devil live wherever it wants? Garbage, why am I visualizing a stupid myth. A myth with hairy blue legs, hooves for feet, black horns that round in a crescent circle, human mid torso and human arms, but blood red skin. It would possess extra rows of fangs for teeth, like a shark.

Rosa then heard breathing from behind her. The hair on her neck stood up. The breathing was coming in her direction and fast.

Rosa crawled faster into the center of the Godforsaken cliff.

Why did I go along with this?

The breathing gained on her.

Freaky! How can something with human hands and hooves for feet catch up to me. Maybe it isn't crawling, maybe it is short enough to run through the tomb tunnel. Stupid Jake has me thinking 'tomb tunnel' now. Wait, if it has hooves it would be galloping, not running.

She crawled faster.

"Ouch! No, ewww!" her hand hit something sharp and fuzzy. Jerking her hand back she paused to inspect it. She could feel the wet stickiness from blood.

I definitely cut it. Hopefully not bad?

Rosa went to hit the flashlight to see if she could get it to work, at the same time a hand grabbed her ankle. Rosa let out a howl, whipped the flashlight around so quickly she clonked whatever grabbed her.

"OW!"

The flashlight flickered on.

"Cody?"

You are so cute.

Cody faked exaggerated pain as he rubbed his shoulder. Every muscle in Rosa relaxed.

Too bad you are Scout's brother. I would have thought you might like me if I didn't know you're only here because you're forced to be around me.

"Mom's rule number one, never go anywhere alone. That includes creepy tomb tunnels," Cody whispered.

Rosa breathed a sigh of relief, "I thought you were the Jersey Devil."

Heck, I would have volunteered to do this if I knew you were going to crawl in here with me. You're always so nice to me.

Cody continued explaining, "Besides this is all my fault. I was trying to pick on Scout not you. Max would have volunteered in a minute to crawl in here for Scout if she lost at manhunt. I never meant for you to lose. You didn't have to hit me though."

Rosa giggled.

"Wait why would the Jersey Devil be in New York?" Cody asked.

There, sitting in the palest glow in Tomb Tunnel, Rosa sighed.

This couldn't be going better. Maybe Cody might actually like me.

"We have to be near the end of the rope. Can you hold the flashlight so I can examine my hand?" she asked. Rosa leaned in, pressing her arm against Cody's to position her hand right under the flashlight.

Should I turn my head and kiss him? His cheek is inches from me. Would he get mad if I kiss him? I never kissed anyone before.

"It doesn't look that bad, but it may be difficult for you to keep clean while we crawl."

Cody started feeling her hand, and asked, "We have plenty of evil things in New York, without needing New Jersey's evil."

"You mean like Old Man Brimmer," Rosa asked, while feeling a slight cross breeze.

"Let's not talk about him," Cody said, laughing. "In fact, let's not talk about that stuff at all."

Just then the breeze whistled, and the flashlight went out.

"Wow, I picked this flashlight special for you because Dad said it was his lucky flashlight," Cody said. "This is a really baaaaad flashlight. Wonder why it is his favorite?"

Rosa, still sensing the warmth of Cody's face turned and kissed him ever so softly on his cheek.

Cody said, "Hey, I have Ted's phone. He set it so it is recording video, but we can switch it to one of those flashlight apps. Do you know how to work this thing?"

Rosa melted.

I kissed him and all he can do is talk about a flashlight app. I'm so stupid! Cody doesn't like me. I bet they pressured him to follow me for the dumb YouTube channel. Jake probably put him up to this.

She turned continuing her crawl into the darkness, fast and confused. Before Rosa knew it, the end of the rope pulled tight.

Crap why can't I escape. I am so embarrassed. Cody was just being nice and I confused it with liking me. Why am I wrong about everything? Why couldn't tomorrow be here.

Cody caught up to Rosa, bumping into her enough to knock her sideways onto her butt, not seeing her in the darkness.

"Hey, what's wrong? Did I say something?"

Thank goodness the flashlight isn't working. Cody is cute, but it was really stupid of me to think he likes me.

Hiding her feelings in the inflection of her voice, she responded to Cody, "Besides the fact that we are crawling through a pitch-black cave in the side of a cliff loaded with rats, snakes and skeletons? Plus, I cut my hand?"

Cody hit the base of the flashlight extra hard. It flashed on long enough to locate Rosa's face. Then the flashlight went out again.

"What is that? Rosa, stay still."

What did Cody see? Was there a snake right above her? Was it Old Man Brimmer? Maybe this is where Old Man Brimmer hides the bodies of the children he stole, and their skeletons are all behind me.

Rosa was about to whisper to Cody when she felt the warmest gentle touch on her cheek. Cody kissed her.

Wait was that a kiss? Oh! No! Do I ask him? That would be humiliating! What if I'm wrong again?

Rosa whispered, "Cody?"

Cody whispered back from right next to her ear asking, "Are you crying?"

Rosa didn't say anything.

Cody really just kissed me! I'm not wrong? He does like me?

Feeling the warmth of Cody's face with her hands, Rosa turned and kissed him this time on the lips. Pulling back ever so slightly she could feel his lips turn upward into a smile. They sat there not speaking for a moment.

Rosa felt the rope tug slightly then it gave a full yank.

"We have to go," she whispered. The flashlight decided to start working again.

Giggling, both started the plight of the crawl back out. Since the flashlight finally lit the way, Cody acted for the video.

"I, Cody Sweet, am following the bravest person I've ever met. Ahead of me— crawling— is Rosa Murphy. She has crawled fifty feet into the side of the Palisade Cliffs, into the 'tomb tunnel,' as her brother Jake deemed it. She is a modern-day DEAD RINGER." Rosa looked over her shoulder, smiling.

She stopped to describe the cobblestones on the walls for the video at the same area where the small pile of bones from a decayed rat laid on the ground. Cody pointed the phone at the remains.

Rosa spoke, "This skeleton with the little bit of hair remaining is what I cut my hand on. In future tomb tunnel searches, I will be sure to have a better flashlight."

The rat remains made Rosa queasy.

I wonder how many diseases I just exposed myself to.

Squeezing her hand to make the blood flow, Rosa held it up for the recording "If not, you risk cutting your hands on rat remains like I did."

That quick squeeze made dark red blood flow straight from her palm to her wrist.

Sam will like the bloodied hand on video.

Rosa continued, "It was simply a dead rat, which is nothing compared to the harm poltergeists could have done to me, especially if they haunted this very tunnel." She wiped her hand clean on her T-shirt, "Better to have stains than an infection."

Using the flashlight Rosa pointed out the cobblestone on the walls and top of the tunnel.

"This had to be made during colonial times. Look at those stones."

When she scanned to the other wall to illustrate the size of the tunnel, she saw a gap. She felt a draft again.

"There is a connecting tunnel," Cody said. The connecting tunnel looked about the same size, but traveled at a forty-five-degree direction. The two of them had crawled right past it when they didn't have a working flashlight.

"Where does this go?" Cody asked out loud, specifically for the video.

As she sat on her knees, Rosa held her left arm out straight pointing with the flashlight at the center of the tunnel. As she did the draft started blowing her long straight hair back. She slowly looked toward Cody. Cody in the softest voice said, "Whatever you do, please don't say 'THEY'RE HERE,' or I'll pee my pants."

Rosa had no idea what Cody meant. She continued on, making sure to illustrate on video, the tunnel walls were also secure cobblestone. Rosa then suggested, "It's a tomb tunnel for another day."

As Rosa and Cody emerged from the tunnel, all the children froze. Cody had blood streaked across his cheek from where Rosa held his face to kiss him. Rosa's shirt was covered in dirt and blood, because as she crawled, she made certain to keep wiping it clean. Both children looked horrific, but both children were grinning wide. In fact, they were the only two who were smiling.

Jake actually looked like he might have been trembling. He turned to Ted and asked, "Do you think they can be possessed?"

Sam looked towards Ted's phone for the video. "I have no idea how to test for ghost possessions. Please comment below if anyone watching this does? Oh, and click the like and subscribe buttons if you want to see more videos."

Scout, whose face looked all puffy, became defensive.

"Rosa is not possessed! Rosa, Jake claims he heard you scream? Then a minute later the rope started pulling full speed ahead. I was so afraid something grabbed and was dragging you back into their lair from hell!"

Rosa smiling replied, "No, it wasn't at all like that." Crossing her fingers, she continued, "It wasn't scary at all. There wasn't even a hint of snakes. In fact, I don't think they have ever been in there, or we wouldn't have seen the decaying rat corpse. There is an intersecting tunnel, though."

Scout gushed, "No snakes at all! I get to explore the intersecting tomb tunnel."

Ted said, "Let's wait to do another tomb tunnel video. The not knowing what was going on with you two was a little too much for me to take."

Rosa had a heck of a last day playing with the Sweet children. Her grandpa planned to drop her off in Leonia, New Jersey the next morning, to spend the remaining three days of her vacation with her Grandma Mary, her grandma from her mom's side of the family. Then her grandpa would pick her up during the trip to the airport with Jake and Ted.

Rosa even convinced Ted to let her borrow his phone. Ted had never been without his phone before. Ted's anxiousness made him irritable. He told Rosa who she should and shouldn't respond to if he received texts or calls. "Definitely take my mom's calls, and..."

Jake, reaching way up, patted Ted on the shoulders interrupting, "There, there, it will be okay Ted. It's only three days."

Rosa was one of three people to be trusted with Ted's phone. The other two were his parents and he didn't have an option of denying them. No way would he have extended that privilege to Jake. To Rosa the three days flew by way too fast. Before she knew it, Grandpa was picking her up with the boys to head to the airport.

During the car ride, Ted silently watched the video Rosa captured of Grandma Mary's story and almost teared up. The rest of platoon Cramer-Murphy, not knowing he watched the video, joked, attributing the tears to an addiction with his phone. Sensing how personal it was to Rosa, he let them have fun at his expense.

Even with the short distance from Leonia to Newark Airport, Grandpa's driving gave them plenty of time to laugh.

Totally worth it!

Rosa gave Ted a glimpse of why she loved food. It in turn had nothing at all to do with food, but everything to do with the deepest compassion he had ever witnessed. The one that Rosa had for her aging Grandma Mary.

Jake, excited about the flight back, explained the JetBlue plane their flights were booked on, a newer Airbus A320, has the TVs built into the back of seats. He could still get TV time in before German Tiger Mom got them back in her clutches.

Rosa couldn't have had a better vacation. She hated to admit it, because she loved visiting her grandmother, but she missed her brothers. Having Ted along made the vacation much better than being stuck with just Jake. He even stuck up for her when Jake got mean at breakfast. Ted even trusted her with his prized possession, his phone, for the last three days.

The TVs on the JetBlue flight were showing CMN news. Jake glued himself to them anyway. Jake tried to warn Ted to savor every last moment of TV watching.

"After vacation, German Tiger Mom becomes like a MIG aircraft on Red Bull," Jake said emphatically.

Ted, bored with news, said, "I saw a Lockheed SR 71 Blackbird at MacDill AFB." This got Jake's attention. He then asked, "Do you think it is faster than the North American X-15?"

Wanting nothing to do with airplane talk, Rosa spaced out, staring at the TV. The news had a cute boy the twins' age, with a politician talking about something called Community Charter School Program. The boy then leaned towards the microphone and said, "Us cool kids call it CCSP."

Remember to ask Mom about CCSP.

Hunter spent the rest of his summer at his father's side, being pampered. He ended up on TV more times than he could count. The people who worked for his dad provided him practically everything— car service, food, speeches, heck there were even people who bought clothes for him. He found if he used a demanding tone, he could get almost anything, like a bowl of skittles just the green ones. The only thing people couldn't provide him was his dad's attention. He would be right next to his father for hours, but his father would be distracted talking on the phone or reading.

Hunter created a game to see if he could top the previous day's word count from things his father would say to him. He started going out of his way asking his father random questions. Hunter learned quickly that open-ended questions would at least score him five words, where close-ended questions would never account for more than one word. The game came to an abrupt halt when his father barked at him, "You remind me of your mother with all your questions."

I can't wait to start school back up. Wonder where Mike is?

7

EMBALMED BEEF

Vacation was over. Lessons began almost as soon as the plane touched down. Fueled by the reprieve, German Tiger Mom kicked it into fifth gear. Jake and Ted loved the era in history GTM planned. The era focused around the Spanish-American War. 1898 to be exact.

"Old Port Tampa was really the primary staging area for the war?" Ted asked.

History surrounded them which gave platoon Cramer-Murphy a great way to stay close with the Sweet children. All seven children shared a login and password allowing them publishing access to the YouTube channel SSweet1776. Nothing prevented them from making ghost videos while home in Tampa. Rosa was double excited to keep in contact with Cody. Focused on her passions, she even found a way to relate the Spanish-American War to food and add in the ghost twist.

GTM—being surprised by Rosa's interest—suckered Charlie and Malcolm into participating in the children's video. Jake pressured Uncle Malcolm, their father, and Ted to dress in full camouflage with painted faces.

Ted agreed to be one of the fake ghosts in order to level out the contrasting height difference of Charlie and Malcolm. Both men were muscular, but varied when it came to height. Charlie was five feet ten inches tall, and Malcolm soared over him at six feet, three inches.

The children, picking on their father's Irish skin, handed him a tin of shoe polish.

"Dad even zombies have more pigment to their skin than you," Jake said.

"Uncle Charlie, Jake's right. We aren't going for a Casper the friendly ghost look," Ted explained.

They wanted the appearance of shadow like ghosts in the video and, the pale glowing whiteness of Charlie Murphy's skin contrasting with the camouflage face paint wasn't working. He would stand out too much as a living human face. However, putting shoe polish all over his face wasn't about to happen.

Charlie refused to use more than the camouflage coloring, "I promise I will hide my face from the camera. I will simply look down staring at my feet when I walk."

"I'm glad you children have zero understanding of black face," Malcolm said, looking at Charlie, laughing. "If a video of you with shoe polish on your face goes viral, you'll be Court Marshaled and dishonorably discharged by the end of the week."

Being a full family affair, Rosa made certain her script included everyone. Platoon Cramer-Murphy set out right around twilight— which was 8:00 p.m. in Florida during August. "Twilight is the time of day that plays tricks on people's eyes," she said.

"And being the resident cell phone expert, I'm pretty certain that will translate on video," Ted added. They drove up a road called Interbay Boulevard to old Port Tampa, ending up at a state park called Picnic Island eight miles away from where they lived.

Having never researched the history before, that whole area became new, as if being seen for the first time. Interbay Boulevard had seven old houses, designated as historic homes, that were around during the time of the war.

"Theodore Roosevelt stayed in one of the homes!" Rosa explained.

"Hey! Ted, I bet the two of us could get those boards to move," Jake said while looking at two abandoned buildings right as Interbay Boulevard curved away from Westshore Boulevard.

GTM ended that escapade saying, "Malcolm extended permission to punish you same as he did for me to be allowed to teach you, Ted."

"I didn't say a word GTM. Crawling through creepy old buildings isn't my thing anyway," Ted said winking at Jake.

"The historic houses are kept up real nice, so I'm filming it all in black and white. This will help them appear aged. I also plan on editing the footage to only take up three minutes of video, while I do a voice-over, introducing their topic with the main facts on the war. This will allow me flexibility to hit a three-minute mark."

Ted stared down talking to everyone, but messing with the camera app on his phone while he did.

"There was something Sam and I read that said the most watched videos are under ten minutes, so it will help us stick to that time."

"You realize you kids are learning much more than history making these videos, don't you?" GTM asked.

The three children glanced back and forth between each other.

How is this learning?

"Don't listen to her kids. People don't go to parks to learn they go to have fun. Isn't that right, Honey?" Charlie said with a stern inflection.

Once at Picnic Island, Ted handed GTM his phone, and tasked her with videoing. To the viewer, it would appear Ted still had possession of the phone, walking with Rosa and Jake. Ted then snuck off with their dads to pretend to be ghost soldiers haunting the park.

Rosa did a transition, knowing Ted would piece it together later.

"Now that Ted has told you the basic facts of the war, let me explain the untold part. Greedy Brigadier General Charles P. Eagan was the residing Commissary General of Substance. Having never fought a war in the tropics, our government trusted him to be the expert on sourcing food to supply to the troops.

"The Brigadier wasn't an expert though, and he didn't care about the troops. Even though places like Puerto Rico didn't need beef imported, Brigadier Eagan forced them to anyway. See, the Brigadier made corrupt deals to help line his pockets and profit off of the beef our government bought to feed the troops.

"To his dismay there was another man, Army General Nelson A. Miles, who wasn't going to let him get away with it. General Miles opposed the greedy Brigadier and brought all types of attention to the situation, causing other government officials to get involved. It resulted in what is now known as the Embalmed Beef Scandal.

"Reacting to the criticism from General Miles, Eagan heaped contempt on his superior officer, telling the commission that

Miles should be barred from polite society shaming him, which was a big thing back then.[5]

"The Brigadier hated General Miles, and said all types of slanderous things. General Miles couldn't stand by though. He had honor. It wasn't about the corruption in government or the money the Brigadier made. It was about soldiers dying.

"See, some of the meat sent was canned, but most was re-frigerated. A total of 327 tons of the refrigerated beef was treated by chemicals that kill people. General Miles was even quoted saying the meat had an 'odor like an embalmed body.' The soldiers had no choice—you ate the meat or starved to death."

"Despite all the Washington power Brigadier Eagan had, once General Miles got the Embalmed Beef Scandal started, the Brigadier was going to have to answer for his crimes. Brigadier Eagan was brought before the Beef Court. Yes, there was such a thing as a Beef Court. The court only tested the canned meat, not the refrigerated meat. The canned meat was never proven to be mishandled.

"The Brigadier only received a slap on the wrist and was told he was wrong for experimenting on the meat. Ultimately, President McKinley placed Eagan on two years paid leave, then forced him to retire early. Men died and all the Brigadier got was early, paid-for, forced retirement.

"President McKinley was then assassinated, which led to President Theodore Roosevelt's taking office. Roosevelt fought firsthand in the Spanish-American War. He even stayed in one of those houses Ted showed you. More important, Theodore Roosevelt was once one of those soldiers who had to eat the beef. He knew the real truth and took steps to prevent future situations like that from ever happening again. Under his ad-ministration the Pure Food and Drug Act and the Meat Inspec-tion Act were enacted."[6]

Jake's transition began with walking along the thin beach front. He said, "General Miles never got revenge for what Brigadier Eagan did. Here at Picnic Island, we are at the tip of what should be Old Port of Tampa. This is where the soldiers would march before they boarded ships launching off to the war.

"Hauntings by apparitions of General Miles' Ghost Army happen throughout Old Port Tampa. More reports than ever have been coming out about paranormal activity taking place at this park. We think that activity is General Miles' Ghost Army. The sightings are consistent with disembodied spirits resembling soldiers. Some say you can see them holding their stomachs at times. These have to be the soldiers who died from bad beef.

"Like all true soldiers, they once yearned to fight for our freedom. That chance was snatched away from them by their own government when they ate the bad beef. A person that dies that way is in too much peril to move on. Those soldiers lost their lives even before going into battle, which explains why they linger haunting here—yearning to ship off to war."

GTM panned the phone around, searching, then returned it to following behind the children.

Jake continued, "About five years ago the mayor of Tampa made a grave mistake. With the desire to have the nicest parks, he installed a frisbee golf course here on Picnic Island. During the course installation, white one-foot crosses that served as grave markers were removed. No one ever knew whose graves those crosses marked, they had been there for so long. No one should ever remove grave markers anyway. Most people thought those crosses might have been the grave markers of the poor dead soldiers. Removing the crosses spawned extra paranormal activity." Stopping short, Jake pointed.

Three tall shadows of men were off about twenty feet ahead. They looked creepy. Their outlines weren't even visible, due to the way the shadows played. The figures were marching in a line, cutting through to the mangrove trees.

Ted and our dads are doing a great job.

"It's them!" As soon Jake said it, the men disappeared from sight.

"The mangroves are very dark, but let's go see if we can spot them again. I don't think they vanished yet."

Jake ran to the section of mangroves where the ghosts appeared to be marching. He pointed to the trail.

"Weird! They are marching directly into the water."

Rosa added color, "Jake, are they marching paths from years ago? If so, they may haunt parts of the beach that eroded."

"Great point Rosa. I wonder if spirits haunt in the current time frame, or in the time frame they died."

Since the group did not want to walk in the water surrounding the mangroves, they abandoned the idea and started back to their car.

Rosa then pointed to the top of a small hill. Two palm trees silhouetted against the rising full moon. Three figures appeared—one grasping at its stomach.

Jake took over. "Rosa, over there, do you think those are soldiers from the Ghost Army again?"

The one grasping his stomach—Ted—started playing it up, pretending to fall down dead, then shaking with spasms. Then he rose, did a second spasm and fell down dead again. Ted's outrageousness made Rosa laugh out loud.

Jake turned to his sister and punched her in the arm, holding up the 'shhh' sign of his finger to his lips like a librarian.

GTM admonished, "Hey! No hitting!"

Jake spoke through his hands, "MOM you just ruined the video!"

Ted fake-died all the way down the slope, until he got to them with such an exaggerated expression that even GTM laughed.

As all the family gathered back together, Jake noted, "Ted, you can only die once!"

"Says who? If I am supposed to be a ghost, I might be caught in an infinite loop of dying."

Uncle Malcolm asked with a smirk, "An infinite loop?"

GTM are you turning my boy into an engineering wiz like you? You know I can't afford a fancy education." GTM proclaimed, "Well, if Ted follows in my footsteps it won't be expensive. After all, I may have been making pathetic wages working as an adjunct professor while I finished my doctorate, but I earned that doctorate for free."

"Yes, yes, we all know Mom is smart. Can we go get ice creams before she starts lecturing us on how she gave it all up for us AGAIN?" begged Jake.

"She still can't cook like Grandma," smirked Rosa.

"What a bunch of ungrateful little ghost hunters. Next, you'll be calling me the Brigadier instead of German General," their mom said, smiling.

Rosa then asked a question to her father and Uncle Malcolm that bothered her since she started researching The Embalmed Beef Scandal.

"Why are the two of you in the Marine Corps, if our government will do awful things like feed their own soldiers beef that might kill them?"

Uncle Malcolm answered with, "Good question."

Charlie, knowing a question like that from his daughter couldn't go unanswered explained, "America is the best government in the world. Our founding fathers provided us the Constitution to serve as a backbone for this great nation.

"They were smart, unselfish men. They knew evil would always exist. That is why the Constitution is so important. It is a document written by brilliant, God-fearing men to protect the citizens of this country from evil. Even the evil that resides in government.

"It does that by ensuring our God-given rights will not be infringed. Malcolm and I feel privileged to be able to work in jobs that are the first line of defense, protecting the only nation governed by that great document."

Malcolm added, "Rosa, no matter what you do or where you go, there is always going to be evil.

"Being a part of government is powerful. Power always attracts evil. However, no matter where evil resides, good people have to do what they can to protect our freedoms, as prescribed by God, residing in the Constitution. So, yes, the government makes mistakes, but it does more good than it does bad and, even though it isn't perfect, it is the best in the world."

GTM, always having to make things a learning experience, added, "Rosa do you think when President Theodore Roosevelt established the Pure Food and Drug Act, and the Meat Inspection Act, he was trying to do a good thing, or a bad thing?"

Rosa answered, "Good, of course!"

"Today's version of those acts are the U.S. Food and Drug Administration. That bureaucracy has grown so big and has gotten so off course that if a person was dying with cancer and there was a treatment that a drug company came up with that had been tested, and may already be used in other countries, that person here in our country wouldn't be able to use it if it hasn't completed a ridiculous lengthy process for formal FDA approval. Worse, the pharmaceutical company or doctor whoever told them about it would be fined. Even if that drug could save their life."

GTM continued the learning lesson. "Ted, does the term 'Founding Fathers' refer to the Framers or Signers of the Constitution?"

Ted responded, "That's low, trying to trick the new guy. It can refer to both the fifty-five Framers, of which thirty-nine signed the Constitution. However, if you want to be specific 'the Signers' is a term used for the folks that signed The Declaration of Independence, and there were fifty-six of them with only six men who signed both documents."

Rosa rolled her eyes saying, "Does everything have to be a quiz, General?"

GTM replied, "To show you there is value in knowing your history, I have two last questions for you, Rosa. If you can answer them correctly, we will have lunch at that restaurant you always ask about in downtown Ybor."

Rosa stopped still with a shocked expression, "The Bogota? Oh, my gosh! That restaurant has been around since 1905. It is the oldest restaurant in the state of Florida. Please can we just go, even if I get them wrong?" Rosa begged.

Both Malcolm and Charlie burst out laughing. "Rosa, I will explain after you answer why we are laughing. It has nothing to do with you and everything to do with your mother."

GTM asked, "How many Amendments to the Constitution are there?"

Rosa answered, "Twenty-seven." *That was an easy one. Halfway there!*

GTM then asked, "Can you tell me all the things the First Amendment ensures?"

Rosa, bright-eyed, answered, "The right to free speech, freedom of religion, free press, and freedom to assembly."

GTM smiled. Rosa knew they were going to The Bogota.

GTM continued, "The first amendment also guarantees us the right to redress the government. Congressman Harris is hosting a speaking event at The Bogota in Ybor next Tuesday. He has been the main pillar pushing through this stupid Community Charter School Program."

"Mom, cool kids call it CCSP!" Rosa said.

"Oh really? Cool kids? Where did you learn that?" GTM asked.

"The news showed it on the TV on the plane."

Charlie said, "Rosa, we were laughing because Congressman Harris is daring to push a bill that goes against your mother's core beliefs. He is going to regret the day he ever elected to cross paths with this Momma Bear, and I am sure many other mothers have the same strong feelings about the education of their children."

Uncle Malcolm, still laughing, couldn't help himself, "Ted you better use that fancy phone of yours to record the whole thing. The guys back at work don't believe me that Charlie is a pussy cat compared to GTM when she gets the German General attitude going."

Charlie, laughing in agreement, suggested, "Let's title it 'German General Godfathers Government Garbage.' How is that for an alliteration example, Honey?"

Knowing the men had zero understanding of the language, GTM started speaking to the children in German to tease back. Ted, still new at learning the language, smiled anyway knowing her tone, and picked up on a few words including 'hanswurst,' which means buffoon.

GTM became serious. "You realize with only a few hours of TV watching, that jerk Congressman Harris was able to influence your children? Imagine what he has done with the uninformed public. Darn right I am going to use my First Amendment Rights on him, and it won't be to say, 'Bless your heart!' Laugh all you want! I should make the three of you walk home after trudging through the salt water earlier. There will be no muddy boots allowed in my car."

Charlie wrapped his arms around his wife. "Wow, you soured fast, Honey. We aren't laughing at you. We know how important the children's education is. Congressman Harris isn't going to get Florida to adopt the CCSP bill, and even if he does, I am sure there will be a provision in there for homeschooling.

"Besides, you always lecture on looking for the good in people. At least the Congressman likes spending time with his son. Now, I get making us walk for teasing you, but who walked through water?"

Jake looked at the three sets of feet with wide eyes. He said, more telling than asking, "YOU DIDN'T WALK INTO THE MANGROVES?"

8

GOING TO BOGATA, BRING BAIL!

Ted replayed the video of the 'ghosts' walking into the mangrove trees over and over and over again. He even uploaded it for the Sweet children to check out. There was nothing there, or at least caught on video. Jake began to wonder about Rosa's story on The Embalmed Beef Scandal.

"Rosa, did you make up part of that story? Like mostly, the part about soldiers actually dying?" She shook her head 'no' at him.

Reporting wasn't easy back in then. Since the story was loosely based on factual events, could it be possible they really saw ghosts? Even Mom saw them.

"Ted, I'm telling you those ghosts were real!"

If real ghosts can't be seen on video, the SSweet1776 YouTube channel would be a bust.

"We have to figure something out."

Ted figured out how to fade an image off screen on the video, so the children used the footage of them pretending to be ghosts right up to when Ted grasped his stomach, dying the first time.

Sam agreed with Ted. Even though the children used this footage, Sam said, "Faking ghost sightings is only okay for rare occasions. Lying about ghosts isn't cool. Plus, since you already saw actual ghosts, we know they're real.

"BTW, it is awesome that you guys are continuing to create videos. The social-media skills 101 stuff I looked up, says that only five percent of YouTube channels get more than 100 sub-scribers. Can you believe that?

"A factor to success is producing videos on a regular basis like daily or weekly. I can't do that alone. Scout already talked me into a video that had absolutely nothing to do with ghosts or history.

"She had all three of us doing the #GetItUpDanceChallenge. Max filmed, of course. It's so bad! The worst part is, my mom thought it was cute and told everyone around town. Now it is our most watched video by—like—A LOT!"

The children all agreed, they weren't about to stop doing videos because they spotted real ghosts, but couldn't capture the images on video. Sam asked Ted to post all his phone's video footage set to private, so he could practice manipulating the videos. Besides the four YouTube videos posted public which the children had already created, there were now three new privately posted videos:

1. Rosa Hits Pot Head with Board
2. Grandma's Secret Poor Man's Cake Recipe
3. Video of the Mangrove Ghosts

After hours of failing to adjust the Mangrove Ghosts footage, Sam took a different approach. He discovered it might be the limitation in their phones' camera capabilities. He started researching Ghost Hunting and discovered ghosts had to be videoed on full spectrum cameras.

Maybe that was the problem with Ted's phone. That means Max's phone would have the same problem.

Sam knew better then to ask his parents to purchase him a new fancy camera. However, Sam's research uncovered that Electro Magnetic Field Meters (EMFs), as well as Electronic Voice Phenomenon (EVP) recorders, were items every ghost hunter had to have and available rather cheap on eBay.

When Sam tried to convince his father to make a purchase or even open a PayPal account, Mr. Sweet quoted Abraham Maslow.

"Sam, to a man with a hammer, everything looks like a nail."

Not sure what the heck that means, but I'm sure it translates to 'no'.

While Sam focused on how to get the proper equipment to enhance the ghost video, Rosa fixated on going to The Bogota. She loved that building, and she salivated in anticipation of the excellent food they serve. Hoping Cody would answer the phone, Rosa called the Sweet house in advance of their trip to The Bogota. Mrs. Sweet answered.

"The children aren't home yet. It isn't 5:00 yet. Of course, I will tell them over dinner that you are going to a very OLD restaurant."

Dang it, not like I can call Max's cell and ask for Cody.

GTM and the three children all arrived at the Bogota around 2:00 p.m. Tuesday as a treat for Rosa. This way they could enjoy eating lunch prior to the Congressman's speech.

Rosa's anticipation grew as they walked past the bright blue and yellow tiled wall along the whole sidewalk block, with traditional beige iron rails leading to the entrance. There was even Valet car service.

The hostess greeted them. "Hi, I'm Missy. Do you have a preference on dining rooms? The only two rooms not available at the moment are those Congressman Harris reserved for a fund-raising event later today."

Jake said, "We are definitely here for him."

The hostess, Missy, squinted her eyes tilting her head, "It doesn't get going for a few hours, but if you have tickets for the $3,000-per-plate benefit, I'm sure we can seat you early."

GTM's mouth fell open so wide it could catch flies. She clarified, "We are here only to see the Congressman's speech, but not the benefit dinner. How expensive is this restaurant, hopefully not normally $3000-per-plate?"

Rosa blushed.

Missy handed GTM a menu, leaned over the hostess stand and whispered to the children, "Your mom is right. Great food doesn't have to be expensive. In fact, many of the same foods the folks will be eating at the benefit dinner today, were served to the protesters of the 2012 Republican National Convention for free."

Ted asked, "You gave your food away for free and to Democrats?"

Odd a teenager should care about politics.

Missy continued, "Yes, our restaurant didn't care if they were Democrat or Republican, we fed them for free out of a deep embedded belief in the right to peacefully protest. They feel the right to protest is one of the great advantages we have, that makes our country better than any other country."

"How do they feel about the right to question the heck out of a pushy Congressman?" GTM asked.

Missy said, "Well, if you're talking about that crazy CCSP bill, let's just say I am so grateful my children are grown. Now, I can't reward you with free food but, I can sit you at one of the best tables in the restaurant."

Missy sat them right next to a fountain as tall as Ted. Rosa looked all around, as if she gazed at stars above her.

This is perfect. There is even a balcony surrounding us where the ceiling opens to a second level.

She had to be reminded to sit down when their waitress appeared.

"Okay, we have about one hour to enjoy lunch. That will give us the perfect amount of time to position ourselves upfront at Congressman Harris's speech," GTM said.

GTM had questions all written ahead on cue cards.

Even though Malcolm teased me for having a German General attitude, I have a feeling he is right.

"Ted make sure Rosa doesn't use up all your phone's battery. Your dad is right, you should video our asking questions of Congressman Harris."

Their waitress, Eva, didn't hesitate to elaborate on the story of The Bogota. She provided a colorful history of the 4th generation-owned restaurant to the first-time diners, going out of her way to answer questions for Rosa.

"The room where you are dining—the Don Quixote Room, opened in 1935 as the first refrigerated, now known as air conditioning, dining room in Tampa. The windmill art on the walls, and bright tiling make it as perfect as Cervantes' classic novel."

Rosa insisted on ordering for all of them. Without glancing at the menu, she rattled off, "We will have the Tapeo Sampler.

The three Tapa dishes we would like are: Stuffed Piquillo Peppers, Puntas De Filete 'Jerez', and Almejas en Salsa Verde." She had even Googled correct pronunciations of the words in advance.

"Of course, we will all have our own slice of Flan." Rosa then said to her mom. "It's a Spanish caramel egg custard. The Bogota has won more awards for their Flan than the number of years they have been in business, and that is A LOT, since they have been around since 1905."

"Please add a Cuban sandwich onto the order. Three small plates will never fill up the two boys."

Eva, overjoyed by the young girl's enthusiasm, explained, "There are actually eighteen rooms within the one restaurant, and it can seat 1,700 diners all at the same time. If you would like, I can show you a tour after the meal?"

Rosa was in heaven. *This is what learning should be about.*

At about the time the family sat down to lunch, Congressman Harris and his son, Hunter, landed in a private airplane at Peter O'Knight Airport on Davis Island. It was a smaller airport, and from the air often can be mistaken for MacDill AFB, since the runways are close to one another.

The Congressman was back in his hometown, after twisting arms in Tallahassee. He had to ensure Florida became one of the early adopters of CCSP. The small airport was less than six miles from the restaurant, but he had to visit multiple constituents and donors for private discussions prior to his speech.

Hunter thought this was the most boring part of spending time with his father. His father, although right next to him anywhere from six to eight hours a day, would always be talking to someone else.

We are literally fifteen minutes away, but I have got to sit in this stupid car. Dad will take two hours before we get there.

Hunter opened his iPad and pulled up his picture of Izzy.

About an hour into what Hunter nicknamed 'the waiting game,' he received a text from Izzy. She had been communicating with him, via text, off and on since they last saw each other in the conference room at his dad's DC office. Most of the communications were prep talk on what he should say at his dad's latest speech.

Hunter had to calm his breathing every time his phone alerted him. This text was different. Izzy was asking Hunter where he was, and knew the exact time the plane touched down.

She's is worried about me.

When he explained, Izzy encouraged him to have the limo driver bring him to The Bogota, and go back after for his father.

Wow! Her text says she's waiting for me.

Meanwhile, Eva was having as much fun entertaining Rosa with facts on the restaurant, as Rosa was having hearing them. She asked another server to cover her tables, so that she could show Rosa the whole tour. GTM not wishing to interrupt other diners as she dragged three children room-to-room, allowed Rosa to go with Eva on her own. Plus, the boys were getting restless and edgy.

"I promise to bring Rosa directly to you after we are done. That way you can get a spot up close to the podium," Eva said.

"Rosa, how many more pictures of food and artwork can you take? You must have well over fifty," Ted said refusing to lend Rosa his phone, tour or not. "The battery is going to die long before the question-and-answer time with Congressman Harris. If you use it anymore."

Eva took her time walking Rosa through many unique rooms, "Those four pieces of stained glass were originally purchased as art from people who made them for chapels. Their cost was in the thousands and that was back in the Thirties.

The original owner who purchased them received so many compliments, he had to add more, of course.

"Whenever the owners would find art they enjoyed, they would add it to the restaurant. Did you notice how beautiful the building is even before you enter?"

"I did!" Rosa answered.

"The Bogota shows the synergy between food and art. I think it communicates that great chefs are also artists. You can't help feel at home in here."

"I know. It's like a dream," Rosa marveled.

"I'm studying to become a Sommelier, and although you may be too young to sample wine, you should know pairing wine with food is also an art form. This is one of our wine cellars. You'd rather see the kitchen though, wouldn't you?"

Rosa jumped at the question.

"Come on then!" Eva headed straight back towards the kitchen.

"Believe it or not, the kitchen was recently renovated to allow for more space. Wow, it's unusually hectic in here." Eva said sticking her arm in front of Rosa guarding her from the business.

"Are all professional kitchens like this?" Rosa asked.

No way I am going to get to see Flan being made. This kitchen is abuzz, worse than a hornet's nest getting hit with a stick.

Eva felt a little let down, since she knew this was the room Rosa was most anticipating.

Doing their best to take up the least amount of room possible, they backed up to a pillar. Their mere presence aggravated the cooks. Then CRASH, dishes shattered, arms flared, and Spanish was being screamed at a young boy dressed in a button-down.

The boy screamed back, "Do you know who I am? You only exist, because people like my father pay for places like this! You're a nobody!"

Eva said, "This doesn't look good."

The cook let loose a stream of curse words in Spanish. Hunter, knowing Italian, was able to get a gist of what was being yelled at him. He turned and in full spoiled brat mode started yelling, "I'm going to get you fired!"

Eva said, "Bear with me one minute, Rosa?" She inserted herself into the situation. It turned out Hunter was lost looking for Isabella and was misdirected into the kitchen.

Eva knew a stern fast rule to working in restaurants, always vacate the kitchen anytime a chef became angry. She told Hunter, "I will take you to Isabella. She most likely is in the Siboney room."

As Eva offered her hand to Hunter he just scowled. Rosa skipped over and grasped her new friend's hand. As they walked, Hunter following, Rosa continued her happy enamored questions.

When they arrived at the Siboney room, Eva continued, "This room normally has performances from Spanish flamenco dancers. Tonight, Congressman Harris is renting it out, though..."

Interrupting Eva's explanation to Rosa, Hunter spouted, "Yeah, yeah I know! He's my father! Now where is Isabella?"

Eva couldn't help think how different the two children were.

One you wished was your own, the other was a pro-abortion poster child.

"Rosa, wait here for a minute?" Eva went off to locate this Isabella.

Rosa ignored Hunter, fascinated by the fountains, sculptures, paintings and tapestries, as she walked to each piece noticing their individuality.

Hunter asked, "What are you stupid or something?" He couldn't help notice the similarities between Rosa and Izzy, but Rosa was ignoring him.

How dare she ignore me!

Rosa just smiled, still admiring a tapestry.

It's many splashes of red and yellow hues remind me of Impressionistic art.

Familiar with taking jabs from Jake, Rosa challenged back with, "You made that chef really mad. I would probably avoid eating tonight." Super ticked, Hunter spouted, "Are you threatening me? Do you know who I am?"

"Sure, you're the boy on TV in support of the CCSP bill," Rosa responded.

Just then Izzy walked in and gave Hunter a huge hug. Noticing Rosa, Isabella asked, "Hunter who is your new friend?"

"She's just the server's girl," he responded.

Rosa retorted, "No, I'm not. Eva is my friend, and she is giving me a tour of the restaurant. My name is Rosa. My mom is outside, waiting to see Congressman Harris speak with my brothers."

At this, Isabella politely introduced herself to Rosa. Her next question was very telling, unless you were a twelve-year-old girl. "Rosa what does your mom think of Congressman Harris?"

Rosa knew she was not supposed to say bad things about people. "My dad, thinks it is great that he is spending so much time with his son," Rosa replied.

I hope she doesn't follow up with, 'But what does your mom think?'

Instead, Isabella asked, "What does your dad do?"

"He's a Marine Corps Sergeant, but he has work, so my mom is here."

Where is Eva? This lady is laser focused on me. Thank good-ness people are setting up all around. Every part of me wants to scream STRANGER DANGER!

Isabella explained, "The Congressman might not have time for everyone's questions after his speech. However, I can ensure you will be called on to ask a question. Would you like that?"

I should head back to my mom. No, I told Eva I'd wait. This woman is acting nice, but I know she's not.

Subconsciously, Rosa stepped behind Hunter the instant Isabella approached her, holding out a piece of paper on which she had written a question.

Isabella noticed Rosa's apprehension. "Would you feel more comfortable asking Hunter a question?"

Rosa looked towards the entrance.

What is taking Eva so long?

Holding out the piece of paper towards Rosa, Isabella said, "I bet your dad would be proud to see you on TV. If you want, raise your hand, and Hunter will call on you during the question time. Here is a smart question to ask."

Eva walked in just in time to hear the tail end of Isabella's request. She saw Rosa, not smiling in the slightest, standing behind Hunter.

"Hey, we'd better get you back to your mom! Here, we can put that right in the book I grabbed for you," Eva said, taking the piece of paper from Isabella and folding it. The book was titled Most Loved Recipes from The Bogota Restaurant. Rosa's face started glowing again.

"Our Flan recipe is the tenth recipe in there!" The two left in search of GTM.

Eva, in her server uniform, had no problems bumping her way through the crowd on the sidewalk, which would soon be closed off. Ybor City closed North 22nd Street between Seventh and Sixth Avenue for the speech. It was a marketing firm's dream setting. The Congressman could pull up to the valet right on Seventh, walk over to the podium for his speech, and then walk off through the grand front entrance of The Bogota to his benefit dinner.

The podium was facing the road, ensuring the beautiful front of The Bogota would be part of the Congressman's backdrop. The sun would be setting off to the Congressman's right. Picture perfect would be the only words a person could describe for this setting, but that person didn't bank on the wrath of a German Tiger Mom.

Eva had no problem finding GTM. She was standing front and center, about five feet from the podium. Eva explained how their tour in the kitchen became chaotic. She then cupped her mouth with her hand and spoke into GTM's ear.

The partial part Rosa could catch was her mom's response, "That's okay. Rosa is a smart girl in those situations, but you didn't have to buy her a book."

Eva grinning said, "I didn't. Congressman Harris did! After all, it was his son that prevented Rosa from seeing Flan from being made, so the book is getting added to Congressman Harris's tab tonight." She then waved to Rosa and went back in the restaurant.

GTM, grinding her teeth, slid the piece of paper out of Rosa's book. The question written on the paper was: HOW SOON DO YOU THINK FLORIDA CAN HAVE CCSP?

Two can play at this game.

"Rosa, I do want you to ask a question, but not that one."

Rosa became nervous, sensing something was afoot. Her mother had that same crooked smile Jake wore when he planned on doing something wrong. "Mom, please I don't want to."

GTM continued her convincing, "How about this Rosa? All four of us will raise our hand, and whoever gets called on will ask the question?"

Ted said, "I'm in. Being tall always gets me called on."

"Nuh-uh," shouted Jake. "I'm going to be called on."

Rosa crossed her arms, "I don't want to. I know they will call on me."

Jake responded, "No one can know that. I call phooey."

GTM put aside her anger over CCSP, and realized she shouldn't trick her own daughter; so, she took the next tactic. "Rosa, I will help you cook all twelve of the recipes in that book next week, if you ask just one question."

Rosa hesitated, but agreed.

I know where Jake learned his tactics.

Except for knowing it was cool to call the Community Charter School Program CCSP, Rosa didn't understand what was taking place. The boring speech wasn't helpful with clarification. All she wished was that no one call on her.

Rosa didn't like the bratty Congressman's son, but she didn't want to embarrass him. She knew the question her mom was making her ask would cause trouble.

Her dad described Congressman Harris as a slippery politician. He said, "He's the type that can get through a locked door without turning a key."

When the Congressman moved on to questions, he called only on reporters. He knew each of their names. Rosa raised her hand halfway up. The Congressman announced, 'no more questions,' and appeared to step away from the podium.

Great. That kid isn't going to get the chance to call on me.

Rosa breathed a sigh of relief, until the Congressman put his arm around his son and said, "Why don't you take a question?"

Nooo! CRAP!

"Okay, how about you, little girl right in front?" Hunter asked.

How come he said it like that, 'little girl,' that's—that's derogatory!

She wasn't going to feel bad after all. Rosa envisioned Scout behind Hunter with a balled-up fist, doing the motion of an uppercut, as a sign of 'Go get him!'

"WHY DOES CCSP WANT TO TAKE ME AWAY FROM MY PARENTS?" She yelled.

Hunter hesitated, "It's not."

Congressman Harris stepped in. "NO ONE IS TAKING ANY-ONE AWAY FROM THEIR PARENTS."

News cameras started focusing on the cute little girl who is afraid of being taken away from her parents.

GTM spoke loud and quick to those cameras, "Five days a week is 260 days a year. That's 70 percent of my children's lives, they will be away from me. You don't even allow for homeschooling. Your stealing our children away from us!" Playing to the cameras, GTM wrapped her arms around the three children.

The Congressman couldn't walk away. He didn't mind arguing with this degenerate woman, but he wasn't going to continue it in the public eye. Doing the first instinctual thing he knew to do with an upset woman, he tried to give her something, saying, "Why don't you join us at the benefit dinner tonight, and we can discuss this rationally?"

GTM retorted, "For $3,000 a plate, NO THANK YOU!"

But Congressman Harris had already walked away from the podium, and headed for the entrance of The Bogota. Some of the Congressman's security ushered GTM and the children into the front entrance behind him, knowing they should stay nearby ready to usher them out the back.

Once the front doors closed, the Congressman did his attempt at rationalizing. He started spouting statistics about illiteracy, and heartfelt concerns for children.

An enraged GTM responded, "So, you are going to sacrifice my children for the good of the many. That's not how this country works!"

Hunter jumped in, "Dad, you told me those people aren't worthy of answering. Kick her out already."

Ted turned the camera that was recording down at his side, from Congressman Harris towards his son Hunter, and asked, "What do you mean by 'those' people?"

Hunter, feeling empowered over the weeks of people doing whatever he said, went on an insult rampage. "Those people meaning your mom who has three kids by different dads. Look at how you're dressed. Shop much at Walmart lately? You are totally the statistic we are trying to help. I bet you barely can read, which is why stupid Rosa couldn't even ask the simple question we wrote down for her to ask."

Jake no longer cared about rules. This jerk just insulted his mom and Rosa. He charged Hunter, while punching in a windmill fashion. Rosa, who had grown used to interfering in play fights between Ted and Jake, instinctively stepped in to block Jake.

It took just one security guard very little effort to contain Jake. The small-for-his-age, twelve-year-old boy didn't get anywhere near the Congressman's son.

With Jake in the security guard's grasp, Hunter punched with everything he had. The security guard holding Jake had already started to move Jake away, though. The punch went astray, and clocked Rosa right in the cheek. She stood there stunned, staring at Hunter. He didn't once utter, 'I'm sorry.' They just stared at each other.

GTM was also in reactive fight breakup mode, yelling "Children, children!"

Congressman Harris barked, "Lady, put your boy on a leash."

"Are you implying I'm an animal! Your son just punched my daughter in the face."

Rosa took the upper hand, "That's all right Mom. I'd say he hits like a girl, but that's an insult to us girls! I'm okay. Let's leave."

The Congressman told Security to escort them out the back. Grabbing Hunter's arm, the Congressman pulled him away, disappearing.

Ted had his phone down by his side now still recording. Just when he thought it couldn't get uglier GTM declared they were leaving, but by the front. Ted turned the phone in her direction. As she walked towards the front entrance, taking Jake by the arm, two security guards blocked her passage.

"Ma'am if you want to leave you must use the back exit." To which GTM turned cross.

"I will leave by this here front door, or you can call the authorities."

Not wanting either situation to occur, a larger security guard grasped GTM in a bear hug from behind. Since she qualified in the light flyweight division (under 108 lbs.), GTM was lifted off her feet without issue.

The children are watching, remain calm! Whatever I do I must protect the children. Don't fight, don't yell, just remain calm.

The children started following, not knowing what to do, but also not allowing their mom out of their sight. Ted inserted his body right next to the man holding her. He knew the recording could do more damage than he could do against six men. He also wanted to be right next to GTM if anything real bad happened.

She's only being carried.

They were in front of the hostess stand again. Out of the blue a security guard said, "Hey, we will take that phone," looking straight at Ted. Ted stopped, glanced back at the wall of security guards, and then at the nice hostess he met two hours earlier.

What Missy said was, "We fed them for free, out of a deep embedded belief in the right to peacefully protest!"

"Missy help!" Ted screamed as he brushed behind Missy.

Missy, knowing the members of the family she just met are 'good people,' acted as if Ted bumped her hard. She deliberately tipped the hostess stand, sending it flying in front of the guards, creating a hurdle for them. Missy pretended to grab for it, clasping at the menus, then tossing them in a fanned-out motion.

The guard who almost had Ted's arm, stepped on a menu with his left foot which slid due east at a 45-degree angle from his body.

Ted was free. He just had to run fast, which he did well. Doing his best Heisman trophy award imitation, Ted pushed through The Bogota's double entrance doors with his left hand out blocking, his precious high-priced cell phone in his right instead of a football.

The glory Ted felt was short lived, as he sat around the corner in the garage waiting for the rest of his family to approach their car. As with the 'tomb tunnel,' the not knowing was harder than all of the worst-case scenarios.

Maybe I get why my dad's always being gone drove my mom away from him.

He didn't want to think too hard on it, but after an hour went by, Ted called his dad. His dad was with Charlie, who was informed a few minutes prior that GTM, Jake, and Rosa were taken into custody by the Tampa Police Department.

It's going to be a long night!

9

THE GREY BAR HOTEL

German Tiger Mom sipped the cardboard cup.

Dang! This coffee is really good! Not at all like that 5:00 a.m. gas station bulk package type stuff. It's actually rich and tasty. Maybe I should have a second cup, most likely I will be back in here in a few hours, once Charlie discovers some thug placed me in a bear hug.

The disorderly conduct charge lodged by Congressman Harris's office against GTM was dropped. It happened long after GTM was arrested behind The Bogota, out of sight of reporters or the public eye. Also, decision not to prosecute came after she and the two children were taken for processing to the station on North Franklin Street in downtown Tampa, farther away than the station one mile away on North Twenty-second Street in Ybor—all which gave reporters plenty of time to disperse after the Congressman's speech.

Rosa held Jake's right hand with her left.

It will make everything worse if I cry.

Her book was clenched in her right hand with that stupid question still inside it.

Why did Mom make me ask a different question? Why does CCSP matter so much?

The children both sat on a steel police bench, waiting for their father. Across from them, in uniform sat a massive police officer, the size of a linebacker. She appeared to be stuck answering calls. She was a thick woman, with short brown hair and a red pigment to her skin that looked like a painful rash. She glared back at Rosa when Rosa tried smiling at her.

Wow, her shoulders are massive! It is way wrong to pick on body types, but she is a lumberjack. Why is she so angry? Why won't she even smile back? How mean! Maybe it's the swelling on my cheek? It must be really noticeable by now. Miss Lumberjack probably thinks I caused a fight.

Jake was biting the nails on his left hand.

What if the police keep Mom? I caused this! That was so bad! The Congressman called Mom an animal because of me! I bet Mom is stuck in a cell with really bad people.

Rosa clenched Jake's right hand tighter, every time a new creepy bad guy was walked in front of them.

"Let up!"

Rosa didn't though.

The heels—that play bad guys in professional wrestling—have nothing on these creeps. Is Mom stuck with these people? Calling them people is a stretch!

An endless parade of weirdos walked past.

The first man barked at them as he went by, making both children jump, then he laughed about it.

The next man had blood all over him, a torn shirt, and kept yelling, "I'm going to suc!" He intentionally walked right into Ms. Lumberjack's desk.

Two more were barely able to walk straight and were pretty much being held up by their arresting officers.

The worst was the one with the police officer who paused to chat up Ms. Lumberjack. Weirdo was hunched over, with long, dirty-blonde dreadlocks down to his waist. His blonde beard was the same long length, but divided and braided. Jake stopped biting his nails to check his own hair's length.

Yup, still nice and short. Is he wearing a flea collar?

Bugs were visibly jumping off the guy's hair. Jake then noticed the braided beard, which was also supposed to be blonde, wasn't dyed red, it was the man's own bloody drool.

Weirdo is missing his teeth.

Weirdo grinned, licking his lips in Rosa's direction.

Who needs ghosts when real humans are this scary?

GTM taught them not to speak with strangers under any circumstances. They sat there not even talking with each other. Rosa looked down towards her book.

If only I didn't talk with Isabella, none of this would have happened. Congressman Harris would have only called on reporters, and we would be home by now. Why, oh why, did Mom make me ask that question? Look where this got us.

The parade of creeps slowed down, but a bearded Hispanic guy in a jean jacket, wearing silver-tipped black cowboy boots, sat on the bench right next to Jake.

This guy must be from a Mexican cartel, or worse, MS-13.

He was Ted-sized big, but older, and he insisted on taking up enough space on the bench to force Jake to scoot, to avoid touching him.

Why isn't he being escorted by an officer?

Jake made it a point to continue looking straight ahead, but did his best to check this guy out in his peripheral vision.

The man smells like the bottom of a dirty ashtray and wore brown coffee stains on his shirt.

The man then turned towards Jake. "Drugs. Do you have any drugs?" he said glaring at Jake as if he was challenging the boy to a staring contest. Jake sat still, looking straight ahead, clenching his teeth as well as Rosa's hand.

What the heck does this jerk want? Where is the police officer who should be arresting this guy?

Not gaining a response from Jake, Mexican Cartel Guy then said, "Hey, whatcha got there?"

Both children remained perfectly still. Rosa winced from the tightness of Jake's grip. Mexican Cartel Guy reached across Jake towards Rosa's book in her outside hand. Jake dropped Rosa's hand, and began windmill punching again. This time his target started laughing at him.

"Charlie, you better teach your boy how to fight."

Charlie?

Rosa turned around to see her father behind them, laughing. Rosa sprang off the bench and ran full speed at her dad. She hugged him hard, refusing to let go.

Jake stopped his hostility. "You know my dad?"

Then, noticing his dad was right there, he also ran full speed into his father without slowing down. Jake added to Rosa's pressure hug.

Jake stopped hugging as fast as he started. "That was an awful trick, Dad." Letting go, he tried his best to regain his tough guy composure.

The two children were then introduced to Paco. Paco was an undercover detective who knew Charlie from the range. He was happy to keep his eyes on the children, the minute Charlie called him.

Rosa's cheek looked awful. Charlie had to have a conversation with a Children Protective Services Officer to explain the situation. While he did, Paco gave in to Jake's insistence and provided the children a tour of the police station.

"So, did you have all those guys walked in front of us on purpose?" Jake asked Paco.

Paco, not thinking, responded, "I wish. No, those perps were all real. Seems like some bad stuff hit the street today, causing the Tweakers to be out in full force, even on a Tuesday. You should see this place on the weekends. It gets much worse."

"Stuff? What stuff? What's a Tweaker?" Jake asked.

Paco continued the tour with more of a 'PG' rating, not answering Jake's question.

Maybe I should be careful exposing the kids to more than their parents prefer.

Nonetheless, Jake listened intently and asked tons of questions.

"How cool!" Jake remarked more starry-eyed than Rosa at The Bogota.

Paco couldn't prevent the children from witnessing a man puke on himself in the drunk tank. He ended the tour on that and walked the children into a lounge area where their mom was relaxing with her feet up, sipping on her second cup, watching the news on CMN. The Congressman's speech was on, but the channel cut off before Rosa asked her own question.

"Gretchen, if you are planning to take on the Congressman, you should find a good source of release for the stress. I would suggest you start coming to the range with your husband. Holes in paper relieve A LOT of stress. It's better than any therapist, or medication. Jiu Jitsu can also be a great help," Paco said.

Laughing, he said, "An arm bar from a tiny little thing like you, and Charlie will have his ego bruised for years. Oh, and Jake, you should check out the YouTube channels Active Self Protection and Mike the Cop, if you like this sort of stuff."

GTM was busy being engulfed in an onslaught of apologies from Jake. Jake took ownership of the whole nightmare. She didn't prevent it, even though she knew the blame didn't lie with him.

"Paco, I did Judo ages ago as a child. I'm not sure it will help," GTM said.

"Not Judo, Jiu Jitsu! I assure you it's different. Besides, they have family packages, and from the looks of it, both of your children are going to need to learn something, especially Windmill Wonder Boy," Paco said teasing Jake.

He continued, "The place is down by University of Tampa. Some real salt-of-the-earth type people from all walks of life go there. It's owned by a guy named Matt Arroyo. Tell him I sent you, and he will treat you better than family."

"Thank you, Paco! My mind was put at ease earlier, when you informed me Ted was home safe.

"The icing on the cake is Jake, taking ownership of this whole mess. Those books I had them read, written by that Navy Seal guy turned author on decency and personal responsibility, must have made an impression. Rosa even sort of took a high road by not punching back at the Congressman's bratty son. This day is going to be logged as a win in my book!"

"As for Congressman Harris, 'For lack of wood the fire goes out, and where there is no whisper, quarreling ceases.' Proverbs 26:20 Harris may have prevented the world from hearing me today, but I'm going to start a fire hot enough to make even Hades sweat.

"It can wait for tomorrow, though. Right now, I am going to enjoy the love of my family, and my delicious coffee."

10

GREEN ARROW

ΓΝΩΘΙ ΣΑΥΤΟΝ

"There is only one Good—Knowledge
and only one Evil—Ignorance."
Socrates

Wednesday morning began as routine as possible. At 5:30 a.m., Malcom dropped Ted off, picked up Charlie, and headed off to MacDill AFB for work. GTM had built the day's lesson plan around Philosophy. The events that occurred the day prior warranted the study of Greek Philosophy.

I may have to be cautious not to scare the children avoiding the similarities with the fall of the Roman Empire and modern society, though. The Congressman's speech can be used to at least enrich the children's critical thinking skills. I'm eager to see how their little minds relate what society just thrust us into, with the lessons from the philosophers.

"How can we continue business as usual like this?" Rosa asked.

"Rosa, I realize you're still nervous about yesterday's debacle. It went from delightful to disastrous, but life goes on."

GTM then quoted Socrates to the children. "Strong minds discuss ideas, average minds discuss events, weak minds discuss people."

Ted instantly said, "Does this mean I can't call that kid Hunter an ..."

"NO!" GTM cut off Ted's statement before he could finish. "You neither Jake!" exclaimed GTM with a smile.

"If you do, you are being weak minded. It is also why we won't be sharing the video footage Ted gathered. Our goal of questioning Congressman Harris yesterday was to open up discussion around the Community Charter School Program. The Congressman let me down by not having open discussion. It is also why we will rise above dwelling on any of the events that followed my questions to Congressman Harris. Doing so would make us average, and we are strong minded."

Ted squirmed, "I sorta already uploaded the video footage to the SSweet1776 channel. They are all set on private though, except the clip of the security guard who put you in a bear hug. None of us were in the video and you are hard to recognize. I made sure to edit it zooming in on his face. This way everyone can see who he is.

"GTM no man should ever treat a woman that way! That had to be shared! I forwarded it to the local news channel."

GTM frowned.

Oh boy, hopefully nothing will come of it.

Then she smiled at Ted. "Back to today's lesson Ted."

"Western philosophic tradition is based on Greek philosophy. Socrates is considered the father of modern Western philosophy, and our legal system is actually based on a line of questioning he created, called the Socratic method. His model of questioning is to divide a claim into three parts; examine a claim, question that claim, and find true knowledge. It is also understood as inquiry thought learning."

The phone buzzed in the background.

"If we examine the Congressman's speech from yesterday, his reasoning for more forced education is that it will resolve low illiteracy rates, thus helping the United States be a more productive society. I want all three of you to use the Socratic method on the Congressman's reasoning while I answer the phone."

"Hey, Honey. I know CMN didn't air you and Rosa asking the Congressman questions, but the local news did. You are one of the few people on a state level that has stood in opposition to this bill. The local footage is now being aired by all the major networks. In fact, it is being shared on all the platforms. Because of you #ccspiskidnapping is trending. You have gone viral Honey!" said Charlie. "You and the children really should turn on the TV for this one. Stick with WOLF News though. You don't want the children seeing what some of those other stations are saying about you."

GTM agreed and went back to the children. She looked at them standing around discussing the Socratic method.

All children should be allowed to learn and exercise their minds this way.

"Are these your answers?" Written on their white board the children listed three questions to help conclude if Congressman Harris's claim of pushing the CCSP bill forward will solve illiteracy:

I. Is illiteracy costing the United States a fortune, an accurate claim? Rosa questioned. "There are too many correlations between illiteracy and less employment opportunities which means more social welfare, for it not to be legitimate. This validates a need to help solve illiteracy.

II. Will preventing illiteracy save the United States money? Jake concluded. "Yes, there is proof enough that if illiteracy rates are lower, the United States could be a more productive society. However, the word 'illiteracy' can be substituted with other words, i.e. drugs. Illiteracy alone is not significant enough to warrant CCSP and there is no conclusive evidence that solving illiteracy alone will make society more productive."

III. Does the Community Charter School Program actually solve illiteracy? Ted opposed. "I disagree with the question. I went to public school in Miami-Dade. It is very different than being homeschooled by you, GTM. CCSP will be an expansion of a broken system. If the current school system is already failing students, how can more of the same result in a different outcome?"

"Great answers!" GTM said. "Our next task is to watch TV."

Holy cow! Did Christmas come early?

Rosa fell down, pretending to faint. Ted and Jake rushed the couch for seating positions.

"Calm down. It is it just to view the news."

The children's excitement didn't waver. If you offer a starving man a piece of bread. That man isn't about to throw it back to demand chocolate cake. WOLF News featured different views from multiple correspondents, all discussing GTM's questioning of CCSP.

The discussions ranged from—an unknown woman scaring her children with lies of a school system kidnapping them—to Congressman Harris assaulting a single mother of three—to the claims that 'a person' like GTM should be grateful for more government assistance.

"How dare you! First of all, I'm not a single mother and even if I were, who are they to assume I'm on government assistance!" GTM said, angry at the TV.

"Mom, they can't hear you!" Rosa smirked.

About the only thing said that wasn't a double-edged sword came from Rebecca Ann, a blonde bombshell in dark-rimmed glasses, who empathized with GTM's concern because she was a mother of five. She fully supported GTM, portraying her as a mother who cared for her children, that went out of her way to question a Congressman.

Rebecca Ann said, "It's refreshing to have someone question the CCSP bill, and if it goes too far."

GTM couldn't help herself—she was a moth to a flame. All these people were talking about her without even knowing her.

To maintain the premise of a learning experience, GTM asked, "See if you can write down any discussion points, claims or lines of questioning that we can analyze same as we did with the Congressman's speech."

Some conversations addressed the speaking event, but not one questioned the bill itself. Three hours elapsed, yet nothing substantial was discussed.

Why isn't anyone talking about the actual bill?

After three hours, Ted admitted, "This might be stretching it, but in a round-about-way the news was implying that 'single mothers should be more grateful for CCSP.' Since they assumed GTM was a single mom, they said, that you should be more grateful, because CCSP gave you more free time to do things like work on your own education. I kinda think that's implying single mothers don't want to spend as much time with their children as two-parent households.

"Maybe if the news thinks single mothers want less time with their children, isn't that saying single mothers love their children less than two-parent households?"

GTM, appreciating Ted's effort, explained, "I fear I'm making you reduce yourself to their level which is only a little higher on the scale than name calling. You aren't wrong though. Three hours of news and nothing substantial was discussed.

"Let's enjoy lunch and move onto Math," GTM suggested.

Ted mimicking Jake and Rosa's snarky ways, did a quick search on his phone while biting into a grilled cheese.

"How is this for math numbers? There are 74.2 million children in the United States under the age eighteen," Ted reported.

Bracing herself in a chair, GTM whispered, "and no one is asking questions on their behalf." Seeing GTM turn pale, Ted apologized, "I didn't mean to upset you. I'm really sorry."

"You didn't upset me, Ted. I truly believe CCSP is not the right answer, and I fear it is doing wrong by children. I was only concerned with the bill because I love you children. The enormity of it set in when you read the 74.2 number. 74.2 million and a news anchor discussed how my hair looked frizzy from the humidity, instead of the actual merits of this bill."

The children then officially experienced the first half-day GTM ever allowed.

"Best Wednesday ever!" Jake proclaimed.

They spent the afternoon with GTM, surfing news channels on TV, Ted's phone, and their iPads, without restrictions. GTM even broke out a mega-sized bag of Doritos. The realization that any substantial claim supporting the CCSP bill would be discussed, went out the window.

"The new goal is to find anything positive said about our questioning Congressman Harris." *So far, only Rebecca Ann defended me.*

The children found one YouTuber, Mark Dice, who is followed by more fans then CMN had in ratings. He had posted a ten-minute video, going out of his way to point out the absurdity of treatment being cast at a mother, because she asked questions of a Congressman on a bill that will directly impact her children.

GTM switched to a movie for the children.

This is teaching them that if they don't conform, when they believe something is wrong, they will get singled out and isolated. I want them to grow up questioning things, especially questioning what is right and what is wrong.

Meanwhile, Charlie Murphy's afternoon took a turn for the worse after returning from lunch at Lola's, an old house converted into a Cajun Louisiana style restaurant, that catered mostly to takeaway food by only offering a few picnic tables for seating. He was called on the carpet by his Commanding Officer for the events that happened at The Bogota.

Apparently, Congressman Harris wanted to flex his muscles a bit. Through Isabella's channels, Charlie Murphy was placed on injured reserve to prevent him from training with his men for their next deployment, pending several evaluations.

Malcolm, hard pressed to help anyway he could, convinced Charlie to stop on their way home from work and pick up a nice bottle of wine for GTM, and let the twins crash with him and Ted for a sleepover at his place that evening.

"She certainly deserves some downtime," Malcolm said. "I also want to stop and snag some beer. Going on deployment without you, Charlie, is wrong, really wrong!"

Charlie Murphy's phone rang, "Hey, Paco! What's up?"

"Hi, Murph. I've got some bad news for you. Can we meet somewhere?"

"Sure. Where?"

"Let's hit the range."

"Sure. 1800?"

"Sounds good. I'll see you then." The phone clicked off.

Before the children left with Malcolm, Jake stood in front of his mom and opened one of their books on Presidents. He read, "'James Madison, our Fourth President, also known as The Father of the Constitution, is quoted as saying, 'What society does to its children, its children will do to society.'"

Extending his mom, a hug, he continued, "Thanks for trying to protect society, Mom."

Ted smiled, "You are a real-life superhero, GTM!"

"Like Batman?" GTM asked.

Rosa snickered giving her mom a hug, "More like the Green Arrow, Mom. He's ALWAYS way too serious!"

Six o'clock came, and Murph met up with Paco at their favorite outdoor range. "Murph, what did you bring today?"

"I've got the Tavor, and, yes, I am going to be one of those guys that names his gun. Her name is Ziva. Hopefully, she can help take my mind off things. Apparently, I'm being stood down for the foreseeable future."

"Murph, I'm afraid it's not stopping there. Our favorite Congressman wants to use the incident at The Bogota as an excuse to fast track your kids into CCSP. They're going to do everything they can to get your children into the program early, because of GTM's national attention." "Can he do that? The bill hasn't even been voted on at the state level. What the hell does this mean?" asked Charlie. "Your children are going to get a surprise, state-initiated, standardized test, and if Congressman Harris has his way, most likely they will be forced into public

144

school which, with where you live, would have them placed at Robinson High School. If Florida is an early adopter of this stupid bill, they may have to start attending as early as December.

"Murph, I went to that school growing up. Unless it has changed, they're going to eat Jake alive. Jake's small for his age as it is, and you know he is going to test two to three levels up. I realize it only is a day later, but please tell me GTM is looking into his learning Jiu Jitsu?"

Paco continued, "When you were at the station the other night, did you say anything to the Child Protective Services Officer that could be misread. I warned you those departments work on a quota system. If they aren't overseeing enough children, or having a certain number of children taken into their custody, their next year's budget gets cut. Kinda like us cops with speeding tickets."

Charlie thought on it. "No, I did as you suggested—short concise answers without leaving any room for interpretation. Gretchen doesn't want this revealed, but Malcolm's boy Ted caught the events inside The Bogota on video. One of the Congressman's guards picked her up in a bear hug, and carried her to the back door before the cops took her into custody. He even has Harris's kid mouthing off and has the video showing that brat kid hit Rosa."

Paco gasped, "Crap Charlie, I didn't know that happened. You two are really bad at this stuff. Don't you know you always claim assault when you get in any altercation—even if you clearly are innocent and didn't even get scratched. There's a case in New York that would have been tossed out if the people claimed assault. Those boys are stuck looking at fifteen years for grabbing some lowlife's fist, while the lowlife was trying to punch them in the face. Seriously, had they told police at that time of the incident 'I want to press charges for assault,' the whack-job judge wouldn't have ground to stand on. Oh, and those guys had it all on video also.

"Don't get me wrong, I don't mean to go off. There are more good people than bad running these systems. It's just, well, you really have to do all you can to protect yourself from the bad ones.

"Child Protective Services has some real Mother Theresa folks in it. Hopefully, they assign one of them as your case worker, but Harris has a lot of pull, so plan for the worst. I get that you don't want to make waves over the video with the kids, but employing security that would do that to a woman is a direct reflection on Harris. You should use that part of the video. The good news is that most likely, Child Protective Services will only administer the exams, and may not have enough to act on."

As they left, Paco handed Charlie a black bag of coffee beans with the American flag on it called Freedom Fuel Coffee Roast.

"GTM wouldn't stop commenting on how good the coffee was at the station, so I thought a bag might cheer her up when she receives this news."

Back at the house, GTM opened the wine bottle Charlie had brought home earlier to let it breathe. She swirled a small amount around in the way-too-delicate glass and took a sip.

Mmm, a smooth medium grape flavor, with a subtle hint of blackberry, a delicate aftertaste, light on tannins. It lacks that oak flavor popular in California. It must be Italian.

Looking at the side of the bottle, she saw she was right.

At least something is going my way today.

She set the glasses and bottle aside to enjoy with Charlie when he returned. He even said he'd stop to pick up a pizza for them on his way home after the range.

For now, I'm going to do something I haven't done in ages, take a bubble bath.

GTM dimmed the house lights and left all electronics downstairs. She even lit a vanilla candle.

Maybe there is some truth to aromatherapy, and the scent of vanilla will help me relax. No more than fifteen minutes into her bath, GTM was still failing to calm down. Her mind kept wandering. Huh—74.2 million children at risk and no one is asking questions. Try to think about anything else. The glow from the candle caught her eye. Maybe I can think about the flame dancing? Too late—focusing on it makes me think of book burnings. What the heck is wrong with me? I might disagree with CCSP, but the disagreement is on how to educate children. Both sides want to educate children. Why on earth would my mind jump to book burnings? This isn't evil, it is simple disagreement.

The garage door opened. Funny, GTM didn't hear Charlie's SUV return.

Maybe I relaxed more then I realized.

Grabbing the extra-long, soft-cotton, pink robe the children gave her last Mother's Day, she headed towards the stairs. As she started to step down, eager to hug her husband, GTM heard breaking glass from one of their side windows. Then another. Was someone throwing bricks through their windows?

She ran back to their bedroom and grabbed a Mossberg twelve-gauge shotgun and loaded it up with 00 buckshot.

Chanting began on the front lawn. It sounded as if people were kicking at both her front door and the inside garage door. Peeking out her front window from the second floor, she could see a mob of people.

One was spray painting her car. He was wearing a mask tucked around massive, lobe-gauged ears.

They must be at least an inch wide. How can anyone find employment looking like that? Heck, I can even notice them in the dark from a second story window.

There were about sixteen thugs in total. About half were wearing the same exact black bicycle helmets.

I could easily pick a target and take down five, okay maybe three for certain, before they ran. How lucky these cowards are that laws are in place to protect them? Do they really think they are just destroying property? Okay, if they stay outside, I can convince myself it is only property they are destroying. Pray they don't intend to harm me.

From her vantage point looking out the window, GTM also had a clear view of the stairs off to her right. She still heard kicking, but didn't think anyone was inside, yet.

They are tossing the garage that is certain.

It sounded like a wrecking ball was let loose in there.

I am still safe, as long as no one comes upstairs. Perhaps with all the lights low tonight, the cowards assumed no one was home. Thank the Lord the children are with Malcolm!

NAZI was the word the creep was spraying in bright red on her car.

If he only knew...wait the spray painter has breasts! That explains the equal lobe-gauged ears, or does it? Maybe our doorbell app is capturing details on video of these thugs. They are all wearing masks, but perhaps there are some other unique characteristics that might help identify them.

GTM still didn't hear sirens. She looked at the clock. A good ten minutes had passed. One of her neighbors must have called by now.

As long as they don't come upstairs, I'm safe. It doesn't sound like anyone is in the house, yet. Maybe they aren't really trying to get in.

Then she saw a lit fuse, A MOLOTOV COCKTAIL! She aimed at the arm holding it.

We shoot to stop threats, not wound them. These thugs will definitely attack me if I run out of the house as it burns. The only safe thing to do is stop the threat. Please don't go to toss it? I don't want to shoot you.

The thug was making a spectacle of himself, twirling around like a Hawaiian flame thrower, ensuring all his friends paid attention to him.

Rosa would be so upset with me for assuming it's a man. Rosa, the children, I will lose everything if I shoot. Congressman Harris will make sure of it.

She started processing check boxes.

Am I protecting myself from a deadly threat? CHECK

If I run outside will the thugs attack me? CHECK

Self-preservation is to shoot this hoodlum, but love for my children overrides it. If I am going to have any chance against Harris, my only option is to run through the thugs.

The spray painter was now making a swastika on the big oak tree in their front yard.

Maybe I can make it past them, I have the element of surprise. They all look bigger than me, much bigger. Okay, decision made. I am going to wait until the last possible minute before running. The thug about to throw fire may have no aim. Maybe he will smarten up and not do it.

The Molotov Cocktail Guy tossed the lit bottle in the garbage can by the street.

Thank goodness!

"Look, dumpster fire!" he yelled.

Ten more minutes elapsed. She could hear them downstairs now, destroying things.

That's what Molotov Cocktail Guy was waiting for. His buddies in the house aren't done. Where are the police?

Molotov Cocktail Guy recruited his friend, and they light up two more.

Running is going to hurt! Most likely they will punch me, but if they get me to the ground that's when it becomes life and death. One kick in the wrong place and I might not wake up. Now that there are two of them, there is no possibility of the flame throwers changing their minds.

GTM watched them coordinating where each planned to toss their bottle.

What cowards would let themselves be manipulated like this?

Sirens. SIRENS! I hear sirens, lots of sirens.

One of the guys holding a Molotov cocktail dropped his, running off. The other tossed his high in the air straight for the roof. GTM shot it right at telephone wire height. It shattered showering pieces of burning glass onto the front yard and the scattering cowards.

Crap, that was as much a reaction as it was intentional. This is Charlie's fault for taking me skeet shooting so much.

GTM placed the Mossberg back in the safe before she went to go downstairs to greet the police. Her hands started shaking against her wishes.

Keep your composure, it won't help anything to be a mess.

Charlie saw the flashing lights as soon as he turned the corner. The whole road was in the process of being blocked off. Police officers were out searching everywhere with dogs on foot.

He rolled down the window ready to explain that he was trying to get to his house to an officer.

Holy Hell! They're all at MY house!

At that he didn't hear what the officer said. He slammed the gas pedal, drove up across the neighbors' yards, and stopped at Mrs. Palmroth's hedges next door.

He ran around them through his front door in pure panic. "WHERE'S MY WIFE? WHERE'S MY WIFE?"

The police were taking pictures of the damage on the first floor of their house when Charlie ran in screaming for her. GTM was standing quietly, leaning against the living room wall hugging her robe tight around herself.

Charlie hugged her tighter than the bear hug at The Bogota. She couldn't hug back her hands were still trembling.

So many times, I was in the thick of battle, seeing the worst of things and my only comfort was of my family being SAFE back home. How the hell could this happen here?

"What the hell happened?" Charlie asked to anyone listening. He repeated himself as his panic turned to rage.

GTM started to explain, but stopped as all eyes focused on her. She looked to the kitchen table to sit down, but glass was everywhere.

Turns out I guessed right on the sound of bricks through the windows, ALL the windows. The lazy cowards didn't even bring their own bricks. They used the paver bricks I had edging the garden.

She looked towards the couch, but the vandals had started on it with spray paint. GTM opted for sitting on the stairwell. Charlie sat right beside her, refusing to let go of her.

With his arms still wrapped around her, he shot off a quick text to Paco typing with only his thumb. Paco quickly texted back: Tell GTM to answer any questions the same as you did with Children Protective Services. They both read the text together. She knew what that meant: concise, to the point, less-is-more-type answers.

Not a problem since I'm almost too nervous to speak. The police officers asking me questions seem so nice. It feels odd being guarded.

One of the female officers responsible for listing damages even made sure to include the wine in the assessment. She asked how expensive it was, trying for a little conversation, discussing how she preferred white wines. To which GTM smiled, leaning into Charlie stated, "It was a present, but I suspect from the taste a very expensive Italian wine."

Paco showed up about fifteen minutes after his text. He mingled with his peers, making small talk, while also comforting his friends on the stairwell. "Murph did you pick up that New York style pizza you were talking about?" Paco asked.

Charlie forgot all about the pizza. "Yeah, it's still in the SUV."

Catching on that there was more to the question, Charlie popped up, asking GTM to remain.

Charlie snagged the pizza and the bag of coffee beans off his back seat which were out of sight of other police.

Paco whispered, "Don't let GTM talk about any gun, or allow them upstairs if that's where you keep them!"

Charlie nodded as he turned, opening the pizza box up to an officer eavesdropping a few feet behind them. Paco snatched the box and closed it. "There isn't enough to share." He took the pizza and coffee back to the stairwell with GTM.

The three sat for the next two hours, eating pizza and sipping coffee, making what amounted to a blockade on the stairwell.

When one officer specifically asked to go upstairs, Paco responded for the Murphys, stating firmly, "There is no need, none of the vandals went upstairs. Now quit wasting effort and focus on catching these idiots already."

Paco sat back down next to Charlie and GTM, "Any chance you two can make it the rest of the week without my help?"

That they could.

11

MAKE HER THE EXAMPLE—NO ONE QUESTIONS US!

"Hey! Rosa! Rainbows!" Ted shouted, pointing to a massive bounce house, extending floor to ceiling. The large red columns squeezed it into the area where blue practice mats would be on the floor of the dojo.

"Honey, I promise to focus on the prepackaged standardized test samples—all three days."

German Tiger Mom left Charlie left in charge of home-schooling that next Monday through Wednesday because

GTM had been invited to speak with Rebecca Ann live in New York on air about her thoughts on CCSP.

The impromptu standardized testing was scheduled for that coming Friday, even though Platoon Cramer-Murphy wasn't supposed to know about it.

A matter of greater importance to Charlie was changing Jake's Windmill Wonderboy fighting technique.

Charlie Murphy had perfect timing when introducing the children to Gracie Tampa South MMA. The dojo celebrated the last day of summer camp. The bounce house was a treat to the camp children for a summer well spent training. Master Matt, who owned and ran the dojo, suggested that specific day to help the three children get acquainted with some of the other students.

Normally, a treat like a bounce house wouldn't be shared, but Paco gave Master Matt a heads up on the family's situation. The bounce house helped eliminate that intimidating first impression a dojo has on newcomers. It worked like a charm, almost too well. It gave Charlie enough time to look around and take an introduction class himself.

The three children and Charlie left the dojo that Monday, each with rash guards and gis in hand. Gracie Tampa South MMA had a family plan, which included unlimited classes for the monthly fee. Charlie ensured he and his children could enjoy every available minute of it.

Being far from injured reserve, Charlie had to find another way to channel his energy. Besides, his idea of homeschooling varied significantly from GTM's.

He had three days before she returned.

Charlie had a feeling he was going to need a few Jiu Jitsu moves up his sleeve as soon as GTM discovers the children focused learning on military tactics in the art of war. He hoped the children don't slip up and mention watching the classic movie 'Kelly's Heroes,' one morning to learn about WWII.

Entering the dojo to play in a massive bounce house was one thing, but upon entering the day following, Ted and Rosa slowed their walk. Jake—on the other hand—skipped into lineup position. Master John introduced the three new students.

He then went on to yell in drill sergeant fashion, "What do we first learn in Jiu Jitsu?"

Simultaneously, the other five children in class shouted back, "Rules of engagement!"

Master John continued, "When I call on you, I want you to answer with the corresponding rule."

"Kevin! Rule number one?"

Kevin answered, "Avoid the fight at all costs."

Ted smiled at this rule. "Is there something funny about that rule, Ted?" Master John must have misinterpreted Ted's smile. "No Master John, it reminded me of something my Grandpa taught me."

"Which is what, Ted?" asked Master John.

"He taught me real men have something to lose, and if you can avoid a fight, always do so," Ted responded.

"Real people, Ted," Rosa insisted.

Master John switched his attention to Rosa. "Rosa. After class you will give me ten laps around the mats and ten push-ups for interrupting."

Rosa blurted, "That's not fair."

Using her own logic against her, Master John said, "If you were a boy you would get penalized the same way. Are you saying you deserve less, because you are a girl?"

Rosa responded with a meek, "No."

"Good! Piper, rule number two?"

Piper answered, "If you can't prevent being physically attacked, defend yourself."

"Good! Robby, rule number three?"

Robby answered, "If verbally assaulted, do your best verbal judo to defuse the situation."

"Tim, rule four?" Tim answered, "Control the bully as best you can without punching or kicking the bully."

"Mike. Last one?"

Mike answered, "Submit bullies using minimal force."

Jake took to Jiu Jitsu like a duck to water. He learned the moves fast, using his father and Ted as endless grappling dummies. He even would try his luck on Uncle Malcolm now and then. Each attempt would wind up with Jake lifted by the back of his shirt, dangling from Malcolm's large extended arm, handing Jake back to Charlie with frustration in his voice, "YOUR SON."

The same move didn't work as well for Ted. Even though he was tall, Ted still had some growing to do to catch up to the size of his father, Uncle Malcolm. Jiu Jitsu humbled Ted. He would attempt to grab Jake by the back of his shirt, only to wind up in an arm bar. Size gave him an advantage, but only a small advantage.

Rosa reluctantly went to Jiu Jitsu, until she emailed Scout. Scout emailed back, "Rosa you're sooooo lucky! and I'm sooooo jealous!" :)

Maybe I should try Jiu Jitsu for a few weeks before judging it.

"I'm not going to have a choice on learning Jiu Jitsu, am I?" Malcolm said, as he watched Jake, Rosa, and Ted practicing moves where his coffee table once resided.

"Not if you ever want to hold onto a beer around me again," Charlie said, twisting his friend's arm into a Kimura grip, causing Malcolm to forfeit his fresh opened beer.

With sarcasm, Malcolm said, "You could have just opened the fridge, Injured Reserve!"

"Hey! That's low. What's with the name calling, old pal?" Charlie asked.

"Don't mind him Uncle Charlie, he is just jealous we have mad ninja skills," Ted said, holding up his arms and leg like the 'Karate Kid' movie. He then Chinese movie talked, (forming words with his mouth that didn't match the sounds coming out in the slightest). "You must submit young Jake, or suffer the stinky smell of the rainbow-colored dragon. HIYAH!"

Charlie laughed. "You and Ted will have the condo back to yourselves tomorrow when our window installer is finished. It's lucky Gretchen is off doing that interview, or there would be four of us crashing your couch. Thanks for letting us stay here."

"It's not that, Charlie. They were sending a message! If Gretchen—"

Charlie shook his head 'no' to Malcolm. This stopped Malcolm from finishing his sentence.

"Not in front of the kids," whispered Charlie.

"Oh. Oops! Yeah sure, it's that a year ago it was only me. Now there are five people in my two-bedroom condo. Not that I don't love you..."

Ted didn't allow his father to finish the sentence, as he attempted a rear naked choke hold on him, which Malcolm defended by sticking an arm up to his ear. Distracted by his son, Charlie was able to get a sideways hold on Malcolm's lower torso, picked him up about two feet off the ground, and tossed the massive man onto the couch.

Jake joined in on Malcolm's other arm. The snap of the couch frame echoed when Rosa decided to jump in a seated position on her Uncle Malcolm's stomach. The four-on-one tackling session came to an abrupt halt at the snap, a knowing glance was shared between Charlie and Malcolm, but before anyone could react the couch collapsed.

"Yeah, I am definitely signing up for Jiu Jitsu, especially if Rosa is going to be able to do me in soon." Malcolm said, picking Rosa up over his shoulder as he stood. He then began flying her by one arm and one leg as an airplane, a game she loved, but that her mom insisted she had long outgrown.

"Also, tell GTM, make that two replacement couches she has to shop for at the furniture store when she gets back."

Later that Wednesday, GTM arrived back from her interview on WOLF News, to discover her husband hadn't cracked a single sample standardized test. She fixated on the children's testing and refused to discuss her time in New York. Her silence told Charlie the interview didn't go as planned. The children's 'impromptu' tests, that they weren't supposed to know about, were to occur that Friday, leaving GTM only Thursday left to prep the children.

It was 2:00 p.m., Thursday, when Charlie decided to intervene on behalf of the children. He returned from Jiu Jitsu and walked in to see all three children sitting attention style at their kitchen table, test papers sprawled in front of them. GTM had the children practicing tests since the sun rose. Rosa had chewed off half her pencil.

"She's total German General, Dad. Get out while you can." Jake whispered.

"HEY! NO TALKING!" scolded GTM, as she walked in to see her husband.

"Too late little buddy, but thanks for the heads up," his dad said, smiling at him.

"Honey, you know the test scores don't matter. If Harris gets CCSP passed in Florida, he is going to be hell bent on using these three as an example. He will do everything possible to force the children into the public indoctrination (cough) education system. Heck, he had you assaulted, arrested, our address doxed and me placed on Injured Reserve."

"Are you saying we just give up?" She snapped, on the edge of losing it.

"Not at all. I am saying we roll with the punches and become the biggest possible thorn in the Congressman's side. Six months of public education is not going to kill the children. Trust me, Harris the Horrible will want you busy homeschooling them again, once he feels the wrath of what an angry GTM can accomplish."

The children stared up at him—mouths hanging open all a-gasp— as if he were Superman, saving them from evil Lex Luthor. Rosa risked speaking, "The frozen yogurt shop has pumpkin spice advertised in their window. PP-PLLLEEESSSEEE?"

"Pumpkin spice in August?" GTM questioned.

"Jake was right. You are always thinking about food Rosa, not that I'm complaining" Ted added.

"She was probably fantasizing about organic granola while taking the test, which explains her pencil," Jake observed, the whole family laughed.

"Guess I'm part termite," Rosa said, noticing what she did to the pencil for the first time.

GTM gave a defeated head-nodding approval.

"Frozen yogurt it is! Quick, before Mom changes her mind. Hey! Should we take my SUV or your mother's Nazi car!" The children were piling into the SUV, even before Charlie got his standard greeting hug from his wife.

"You can't always be their friend you know?" GTM whispered to him.

"I know, but frozen yogurt will make you less of the bad guy, as you explain how ugly your interview became."

Jake had an extra-large Golden Toasty Marshmallow and Chocolate yogurt cup, piled on a brownie with so many fixings you couldn't see the yogurt in the cup.

Ted kept his simple with Salted Caramel and Maui Coconut yogurt, topped with tropical fruit gummy bears.

Rosa, being persnickety, built the foundation of her cup with a crisp waffle on the bottom, layered with Pumpkin Spice yogurt of course, with the complementary flavor of caramel chip morsels on top, wedged with two cinnamon ginger snaps to counter the opposite texture and flavor of the salt and spice.

Feeling proud of her dessert creation—and a little overconfident—Rosa asked, "None of this would have happened if we didn't ask that stupid question! Why did you make me ask that stupid question, Mom?"

Charlie's kind nature vanished. He turned parental quicker than they can say, 'Jack Flash.'

He snatched Rosa's yogurt cup, and lectured, "We have every right to question what our government is doing, especially when it comes to you children! I wear the uniform of a Marine every-day to serve my country and ensure the rights and freedoms guaranteed by our Constitution are protected.

"I've deployed to more countries than I remember, to help people in some awful places find the courage and protection needed to question their own governments. How dare the rest of the parents not question this bill? The Congressman should have been surrounded by angry parents in Ybor, demanding answers.

"Instead, he's using the same tactics that I see despots the world over use to subdue their citizens. Do you think your mother asked for any of this? The Congressman is targeting her to single her out, and instill fear in anyone else who dares to think of questioning his CCSP bill. Apologize to your mother!"

Rosa froze. Her dad never gets mad at her. Tears welled in her eyes. "I, uh, I'm sorry."

GTM smiled at Charlie, took one of Rosa's ginger snaps, and slid Rosa's dessert cup back to her. "Your dessert flavor pairings are delicious," GTM said, as a way of accepting Rosa's apology.

"Truth is, I have asked myself the same question, Rosa. Unfortunately, whether I asked Harris the Horrible that question or not, you still would end up going to public school from the way this bill is written.

"There is a vast amount of homeschooling families that are ready to sue the state, when and if the bill gets enacted, but lawsuits take time. The problem with suing is, the case will get tangled up in process, and the next thing you know, ten years have gone by, where the government will just argue that they already have this infrastructure in place. None of which will matter, since you will all be in your twenties by then."

The twins went on to ask Ted all types of questions around attending public school, and he was doing his best to put a positive spin on every answer, but all three children were nervous. Being at school five days a week was scary, even if it was a school close to where they lived.

"If school wasn't bad, why do you prefer learning with us?" asked Rosa.

"I have learned tons more these past eight months than I ever did in regular school. I think half my grades were given to me just because I played sports. What teachers accepted, versus what GTM permits, are night and day different. None of us will have any problems getting A's at public school. That part will be easy."

"So, if that is easy, what part is hard?" Rosa asked.

Ted kept his answer short, "Fitting in!"

"That's because you're too big Ted, you don't fit anywhere." Jake said, laughing at Ted.

"Well, the real fun will be the six months of nonstop Jiu Jitsu we get to do, if you score well on these tests tomorrow," Charlie said, causing all three children to look at GTM with eyes begging for permission.

"Yes, yes, if you do well on the tests tomorrow, we can ease up on book learning, and focus on Jiu Jitsu for the next six months. Since learning from an alcoholic is useless anyway."

"Honey, what are you talking about?" Charlie asked.

"WOLF News got the better of me. I was naïve and believed they wanted honest conversation around the CCSP bill. The conversation Rebecca Ann and I had switched so fast, I thought she was bipolar at first when that 'on air' notice came on.

"Her prep to me was that she would ask why I am uncomfortable with CCSP, and how would I suggest addressing our under-performing public schools. The minute we were on air, her first question was, 'Am I against CCSP because I don't believe poor people have the right to attend charter schools, or guarantee school choice for poorer communities with failing schools?'

"What I responded with didn't matter. I can only guess how bad the sound bites they are going to use will make me look.

"They can rip my responses apart. At one point I said, 'Schools aren't everything' and she clarified my statement, putting words in my mouth, that meant I don't believe in educating children.

"Rebecca Ann wouldn't even let me respond before asking her next attack question. Questions like 'Why at The Bogota did my daughter end up battered and why did I get arrested for assault, if I was just there to ask questions? She insinuated the short video Ted released under #CCSPiskidnapping was a fake.

"Another question was 'How come on a weeknight when children should be at home, yours were playing sleepover, and you were drinking expensive Italian wine.' When I tried to retort, with 74.2 million children are going to be impacted by this, we should be asking questions, she cut me off stating, 'From the look of it, you should be more concerned with keeping custody of your children.' The entire interview, she was aggressive asking me questions, no not questions, allegations, and not allowing me time to reply. It is going to look really bad! I know it is. I fear I failed you kids."

"Mom that book you got me, says, *'You never fail, you either win or you have experiences and learn from them,'*" Jake said.

"Right Jake. That sounds like a long version of a quote from Nelson Mandela, 'I never lose. I either win or I learn,'" Ted bragged. "I have been doing some side reading."

This was what GTM needed to hear. Her children learning to learn without her.

"Actually, Honey, I wish I thought of this earlier, but that treatment makes sense. Congressman Harris is a well-known Republican, who WOLF News has had on as a contributor. The network claims to be unbiased, however, they also have their agenda." Charlie said.

Ted asked, "Aren't teachers' unions Democrat, though? Wouldn't the other networks have been worse?"

Charlie answered, "Yes, they are Ted, and most likely they would have. Consider the Republicans and Democrats to be rival NFL teams. The media networks are fans out in the crowd, and they have a preference for their favorite team to win. Most citizens are also fans in the crowd. The problem is while everyone is cheering for their preferred team to win, no one is paying attention to the game being played against the people in general."

Jake inquired, "Dad, are we talking Super Bowl, or Pro Bowl."

"How about the Puppy Bowl? Can we get a dog?" asked Rosa.

"I surrender! Honey, help?"

GTM laughed that the sugar-loaded attention spans were getting the better of Charlie. "You survived combat. They are three well behaved children."

She paused, waiting for Charlie to try to salvage his analogy. Instead, he opted to eat a mouthful of chocolate frozen yogurt.

GTM rolled her eyes at him and explained, "CCSP is betting on both teams to win. Republicans have been winning voters over by promising to push for vouchers and school choice for decades. School choice makes schools compete with each other, forcing them to be better learning environments. They are in support of children having vouchers and being able to select which school they prefer to attend.

"Democrats have pushed 'busing,' which is supposed to take children from underprivileged areas, poor areas, and bus them to schools that are better in richer communities. You don't have a choice, though. You attend the school they designate for you. Their goal in this is to gain extra funding from the rich areas, through taxes, and claim it will improve the schools. Especially, if the richer communities' children are being bused to the lesser quality school.

"They also use teachers' unions as their strong arm, to rally for better budgets, because teachers aren't paid well. Since teachers are the face of education, this is very powerful. Everyone loves teachers. They are smart people, who chose to go into a line of work that gets paid very little. They go into a career knowing all this, but do it anyway to help children. They are notorious for being kind and having big hearts. Which makes it very hard to say 'no,' when they petition for extra budget money. CCSP is giving both sides / teams what they want, so neither is opposing this bill."

"It sounds like a great thing, Mom!" exclaimed Rosa.

Ted chimed in, "It isn't! The bigger the school, the bigger the program, the easier it is to get by without learning. No offense GTM, but studying under you is hard as heck. Don't get me wrong, you make it fun, but it is harder than anything I experienced in public school. If it weren't for the chance to get to know my dad, I would have quit you the first week."

GTM smiled, "Ted, that is an all-out complement."

She added, "What I hate most about the CCSP bill, is how little time I have to teach you kids what I feel is important. Five days a week straight of school doesn't even allow me time to sit down with you at dinner each night and understand what you are learning."

"UH-OH!" Jake said. "Rosa, you will have no influence over your dinner or the food you eat."

"Mom, I'm NOT GOING!" exclaimed Rosa, as she sat staring at her empty yogurt cup on the table.

Charlie piped up, "Rosa, like combat, you have to focus on the now, but play the long game."

Rosa just stared at him. "Don't win the battle at the expense of the war." She continued to stare at her dad, not understanding.

"The now is relax, and take tomorrow's stupid, standardized tests. I have no doubt we will all be enjoying six months of nonstop Jiu Jitsu after you're done. I even ordered that rainbow rash guard for you, Rosa. Master John is bound to permit a little trash talking, especially when I tell him how Jake is susceptible to rainbows. Just saying..."

12

LIVING WITHOUT TRYING – IS WORSE!

After picking up the children from testing, German Tiger Mom had a new agenda ready for study. She had no doubt their scores would be exceptional, so after testing they headed to Gracie Tampa South MMA. Master Matt believed that even if the Cramer-Murphy children were too old for the 'Intro to Jiu Jitsu' class designed specifically for youngsters under ten, they should still learn rules of behavior before becoming Jr. Ninjas.

GTM asked, "Where did Jiu Jitsu originate?"

Rosa answered, "Japan."

"Eeee, wrong! Brazil. Why do you think it is called Brazilian Jiu Jitsu Rosa?" Jake answered. "Jake you're incorrect. Rosa is right!" GTM elaborated, "Jiu Jitsu's origin was actually the battlefield art of the Samurai of Japan in the early 1800s. It is also thought to originate from Buddhist monks. There were different styles of fighting back then, which are known as ryu—pronounced reee yuu.

"A gentleman named Kano created a style that completely deviated from the others and it evolved into what we know today as Judo. A student of Kano's, Maeda, emigrated from Japan to Brazil. George Gracie, a citizen of Brazil went out of his way to help Maeda, who in turn taught Carlos Gracie, George's son, his style, which is known today as Jiu Jitsu. That's why many think of Judo when they hear Jiu Jitsu. Jiu Jitsu became a Gracie family tradition. George taught the style to his siblings. This was in the early 1900s."

By now, even Ted was glazing over. GTM continued, "Mixed martial arts contests including all different styles were popular in Brazil, but not yet in America. After generations of practicing Jiu Jitsu, the Gracie family had perfected their own Jiu Jitsu ryu. Rorian Gracie, who immigrated to America from Brazil, and Art Davies, noticed the void and developed The Ultimate Fighting Championship, (UFC) that allowed mixed martial art fighters to compete here in the US. UFC had its first challenge in 1993. Royce Gracie, Rorian's younger brother, even though he was one of the smaller competitors, went on to beat four contestants that night and to win. After that, Jiu Jitsu became popular here in the US. Especially, Brazilian Jiu Jitsu taught in the Gracie style."[7]

When they arrived at the dojo, Charlie was there to greet them, after rolling that morning in a no gi class.

Jake instantly blurted out, "Dad, she is ruining Jiu Jitsu!"

Charlie turned to Rosa, "Did you threaten to fart on him when you have him in a leg lock?"

Rosa blushed giggling, "No, but great idea. I might use it on Ted though. He is like rolling with a tree."

Ted, looking shocked and threatened, retorted, "Two can play at that game, and my dad won't blink an eye at me eating beans for breakfast every morning."

"No, Dad, Mom!" Jake demanded.

GTM looked at her husband baffled. "How is your mother ruining Jiu Jitsu?"

Putting his hands on his hips, Jake said with the biggest, most exasperated sigh, "She is making it all about studying, learning-type stuff. Can't we ever just do something without knowing every detail to it? She probably already has massive books picked out for us to read."

The children continued on to the mat to train.

"I guess this is a bad time to tell them that in off hours from Jiu Jitsu we will be reading Musashi?" GTM said, smiling at her husband.

"Honey, what exactly is Musashi?"

"Oh, a fictional book of the most well-known Japanese swordsman who ever lived. It relates because Musashi is supposed to create his own style of swordsmanship. Kind of like the Gracie family perfecting their own style of Jiu Jitsu."

Charlie hung his head, "Unless you plan to hand Jake a sword to wield while you read it, it is not going to qualify as fun. Why don't you leave the next few months up to me?" he smiled.

She is never going to agree to that.

Instead GTM replied with, "How about we start now? You stay here, I have errands to run."

GTM turned quickly, leaving a little broken hearted over not getting to share what promised to be an epic novel with the children. Heck, it was shot down before she even mentioned it was 900-plus pages.

After running a couple errands, GTM found herself in a bookstore.

I'm amazed this place is still here. Most bookstores have gone out-of-business and shut down. Ah, I know why.

The aroma welcomed her in, better than the smell of a Thanksgiving Day feast on a crisp autumn day. The coffee shop encompassed about twenty percent of the store, creating an ambiance of tranquility, versus a standard store 'get-in and get-out' feeling. It was quiet, maybe twenty or so people.

Maybe I could incorporate books about business learning into Jiu Jitsu. Perhaps teach the children the economic aspects of running a dojo. On second thought, if the children wouldn't even like a fictional book, business study won't work. I am going to have to take a different approach completely. Wow, the coffee smells delicious!

Walking through some shelves on sports, GTM came across a book on The Practice of Visualization.

Jake sitting still to visualize anything is almost comical. However, if he thinks it will improve his ability, perhaps he might have the motivation he needs.

Health and Strength was another book.

Rosa will love this. It correlates fitness with food. Now for Ted. He did brag about a championship football game back in Miami. Perhaps something about the steps in performing or winning.

GTM found it, a green covered book, Getting Ready for Competition.

For fun, she walked over to a separate section and picked up the book, Haunted Tampa by Gare Allen.

This book will be enjoyable research for the children's ghost hunting videos. 100% of the net proceeds are donated to the HCSO Deputy Dogs, how cool of Mr. Allen. Oh, it wouldn't kill me to get a cup of 'communist' coffee, as Charlie calls it. Just this one time.

Nearby, a young woman, Isabella, was demonstrating a new phone application, as she sipped a pumpkin-spiced latte.

Greedy capitalism promoting holidays earlier every year. Who cares, they don't hold the real power. Mmm pumpkin spice!

She glanced at her audience— five righteous do-gooders sitting around the table with her.

Sad how they truly desire purpose in their lives. It's so easy to convince them to believe in a cause beyond themselves. University activists are by far the easiest to recruit. Most never had any real responsibilities, not even that of flipping burgers. They never lived outside their own little worlds of academia, gaining them zero respect from fellow citizens. Worse, they lack respect for themselves.

The app was called, 'Evolve,' and focused on recruitment, collaboration efforts, and most important, calls to action. Glancing up for a second, GTM came into Isabella's range of vision.

What pure luck this is! No, not luck, unless you go by the definition of luck the Roman philosopher Seneca coined; "Luck is what happens when preparation meets opportunity."

Nearing the café area, GTM let her imagination have fun. She visualized the aroma of the coffee.

A set of long satin brown gloves were floating out in front of her, motioning for her to follow their lead. The wispy sounds the latte machine was gargling translating to, "Gretchen, come drink me." The forbidden coffee menu looks incredible.

GTM ordered a large, iced-mocha with whipped cream— correction, a 'venti' iced-mocha with whipped cream.

Seriously, as if the barista needed to correct me, forcing me to say 'venti' instead of 'large,' to comprehend what I was requesting. Dessert in a cup, the perfect reward pick-me-up for the challenge of finding something the children will have fun studying, while still physically learning Jiu Jitsu.

She sat down at a table, enjoying her mocha, gaining confidence in her book selections as she thumbed through them.

How inviting this atmosphere is. I should definitely make this a daily getaway while the children train.

Nearby, Isabella instructed one of the activist students, Courtney, to pretend to be a bookstore employee. "Courtney grab a rag and go wipe down tables. Specifically, the one that woman is sitting at. Let's test Evolve." Courtney stood up, happy to comply, until she saw the woman sitting there, recognizing her instantly.

Isabella insisted, "I promise you Courtney, you will be protected. Go! Have fun with it! Make sure she connects the dots. Remember, press the 'live' command to signal the rest of us to help." Isabella then told three of the others, "Go gear up in the parking lot and wait for that signal."

She assigned the task of recording the entire incident to the last student.

Isabella left her latte, and moved over to the magazine racks between the entrance and the café area.

The DIRECTOR is certainly going to be happy with this!

"Wow, that's an interesting set of titles. Are you planning on entering the Olympics?" Courtney asked as she wiped tables.

Before looking up GTM replied, "Oh, gosh no, these are for my children."

"If you can lift them, I'll wipe away those leftover scone crumbs. The man who was here last orders one every morning like clockwork."

How polite! I didn't even notice any crumbs. Wow, the blood red color outlining the girl's nails really contrasts the white cloth in her hand.

"Run out of polish remover?" GTM asked off the cuff.

WAIT! THAT COLOR! I spent hours scrubbing that exact color off my car with Acetone.

Looking up, she saw a cut on the girl's cheek and one-inch gouged ears.

"YOOOUUU!" GTM gasped, clasping the girl's wrist in a death grip.

The girl turned stark white, yelling "HELP! NAZI! NAZI! NAAZZII!"

GTM kept her death grip on the girl's wrist. "Please someone call the police? You are not getting away this time!"

"LET ME GO, NAZI!" the girl screamed again.

The few people that were in the bookshop surrounded them. All videotaping with their phones.

The girl kept screaming at the top of her lungs, "NAZI, NAZI, NAZI!"

"Let her wrist go!" the bookstore manager insisted, inserting himself between the two. He was tall, thin to the point of being emaciated, buck-toothed, had a pockmarked face left over from a serious case of teenage acne, and his breath smelled like he drank swamp water instead of coffee.

"The police need to question her!" GTM exclaimed.

"The police have been called," the manager said, while inserting his body further between the two. "Let her go!" he demanded further.

Before GTM let go she said, "She tried to set fire to my house. She's an arsonist! Don't you dare let her leave."

She then released the girl's wrist. The girl instantly grabbed her cell phone from her pocket, and ran through the front doors screaming as she left, "No I didn't. I only spray painted your car, you Zionist hater."

Using her other hand, the girl made a demonstration of pressing something on the phone and screamed, "You're going to DIE now!"

"Don't let her leave!" GTM shouted again, but everyone stood back, not taking any action.

GTM stood waiting for police. The crowd intently staring at her, slow to disperse. She might as well pay for the books. As she approached the line to the register, the two people in front of her stepped aside silently, letting her advance. People were still recording her as if she was a freak show. She paid without a soul talking to her, not even the cashier.

Standing inside the double-glass-entrance doors, GTM waited for what felt like forever for the police. People were still staring, still recording. She finally phoned in a call to 911 herself. "Yes, ma'am, the police have already been made aware and are in route." Before she disconnected, GTM saw three masked men coming from the back of the parking lot. They had pipes in their hands.

"Help! Please! They have pipes. They are going to kill me!" she yelled to the 911 operator!

Dropping everything in her hands including her phone, but leaving it connected, GTM grabbed the only thing around, which was an umbrella, and wedged it in the door handles. "HELP!" She screamed to the gaggle of onlookers.

This action only prompted the three masked men to run towards the doors. GTM, having next to no time to react, could only secure the doors with that umbrella.

Where the heck is the tough guy manager when I need him?

Pressing her back to the doors, she had to continually turn her face as the small windowpanes shattered one by one.

"Help!" GTM screamed, but people stayed back, watching and videoing. "What is wrong with you people? HELP ME?" she shouted.

Running forward from the magazine section, a tall athletic looking young lady with straight black hair, sprang into action, pushing with GTM to keep the doors closed. A minute seemed like an hour as the men hit at their backs, mostly connecting with the doors and glass. The police finally showed up, sirens blaring. The three men ran. No one pursued them, not even the police.

Between briefly talking to the police and climbing into an ambulance, GTM saw the girl who she thought to be her one ally, holding a latte. Hesitating in her climb, she said, "Thank you," but was interrupted by the young woman, who tilted her head and formed an evil grin.

"You're welcome for my even taking time to give you this option. Stop the noise on this bill and get left alone." She tilted her head to the opposite side, "Get louder, and it gets worse." The woman sipped her latte and walked off. Her crystal green eyes glimmered like those of a tiger about to strike prey.

GTM frantically tried to get anyone else's attention. No one saw the conversation. The EMTs checked if GTM took blows to the head, as she continued to ask after the young woman.

At the hospital, GTM called Charlie and begged him not to mention the incident to the children. Charlie was livid.

Having the house vandalized is one thing, but being attacked in daylight, surrounded by people WHO DID NOTHING, was completely different. How could someone, anyone, not act when witnessing violence?

GTM spent less than two hours in the emergency room, having glass shards removed from the back of her shoulders. ER personnel took pictures to document the injuries, and she provided her statement to the police.

The café must have employed this girl, so they will learn exactly who she is. Her phone records will lead to the thugs with the pipes, and possibly other cohorts as well. With all the video of the girl admitting to vandalizing my car, how could charges not be pressed? Today is a win, even if it was scary. Should I let this all go? What possibly could 'get worse' entail?

Returning to the dojo, GTM saw the children in full silliness, enjoying training exercises that extended from one end of the mat to the other end. Charlie put his arms around his wife, and explained, "Rosa has gotten one over on Master John. She started calling the drill they were doing 'prawning.' The exercise is normally called 'shrimping,' but Rosa insisted that Ted and the word shrimp should never be used in the same sentence. Master John promised he would only call it 'prawning,' if Rosa and Ted won at the wheelbarrow with Ted using his hands to walk. Wheelbarrow was an absolutely hysterical sight, since Ted is so large and Rosa so small. They actually won though."

GTM commented, "Ted must be doing lots of push-ups on his own time, if they actually won."

Charlie then whispered, "I am never letting you out of my sight again."

That night, over a Beef Stroganoff dinner, GTM called an official Platoon Cramer-Murphy meeting. In an attempt to avoid frightening the children, she briefly explained that she was confronted during the day from a pro-CCSP supporter who threatened her. GTM described her as a younger woman with black straight hair and beautiful green eyes. She relayed the options: Stop the noise on this bill and get left alone. Get louder and it gets worse.

Rosa asked, "Mom did the woman wear a green pendant necklace?"

GTM glanced at Rosa, "YES!"

"That was Isabella. She's the one who handed me the question at The Bogota."

"Since none of us can predict the extent of what 'gets worse' entails, we all must agree on how we want to go forward. This has to be a family decision!" GTM emphasized.

Malcolm and Charlie knew their answers, but held their responses, allowing the children to make conclusions on their own with as little influence as possible.

Ted spoke first, "I'm all in!"

How dare anyone threaten my newfound family!

Jake answered, "We would have never started Jiu Jitsu if all this hadn't happened. If louder means more Jiu Jitsu, can I shout from the hilltops? Why aren't there hills in Florida?" he then asked.

Rosa quoted her Grandma Mary, "Good people have to try and make a difference, even if they know they might lose, because living and not trying is much worse!"

Grandma is wise. Boy, I hope she is right!

Ted instantly played, 'Turn Down for What' by DJ Snake and Lil John, off his phone's playlist.[8]

Malcolm started clapping, "Dang, Ted, you can really rally the troops. Now turn that garbage off!"

Jake snatched Ted's phone and hit on, 'Cum On Feel The Noize' by Quiet Riot.[9]

Malcolm shutting that song off continued, "Seriously, Eighties music? That must be your doing Charlie! Let's bring the fight to them. GTM, the trend lately is podcasts. People are craving that long form interview, instead of fake news sound bites. Charlie and I can reach out through buddies. Lots of veterans have podcasts with significant followings now. We are bound to know someone that can help put us in touch, and land at least one interview."

Rosa grabbed the phone.

Charlie wanted to ensure the children knew the extent of what may take place. "You realize, this means the likelihood of being bullied when you attend public school will be guaranteed if we do this?"

Ted said, "Others usually don't bully me, at least not directly. I can ignore when people talk behind my back, so, yeah, I'm sure."

Jake said, "I'm going to try to earn my grey stripe on my white belt by then, so I'm good."

"No way you will do that," Rosa responded. She then said, "Here's my answer," and hit the phone, playing Krystal Meyers 'Make Some Noise.'[10]

Ted stopped her. "Rosa lesson one. When we go to school, NEVER EVER tell anyone you listen to Christian Pop."

Rosa replied, "But that song is great! I'm confused."

Charlie let Rosa's song play out. "Here's a song that helps me when times are bad. I think of you all and the other guys in our platoon when it plays." He hit on Metallica's 'Nothing Else Matters.'

Rosa stated, "Dad, that isn't happy at all. You love us, why associate that song with us?"

"It's not the tune, it's the lyrics. Listen to the words. It is about love for the people closest to you."

13

ANTI-IGNO = YOUNG PEOPLE WHO CARE

Rosa checked her ears to see if they were working right. "Did he really ask Mom that? I love him! Dad, does he really work with you and Uncle Malcolm? Can he convince her to get a Retriever puppy?"

All the children were sitting cross-legged in front of the television, watching the three-hour long podcast featuring GTM and a Navy Seal turned podcaster. He had retired from service and ran a nonprofit focused on rescuing retired military dogs called Warrior Dog Foundation. GTM was being interviewed by him at his foundation in Texas. The only attack question he asked GTM was, "Why the hell haven't you given in to letting your daughter have a dog?"

"Honey, all I know is if I were visiting the foundation, I don't think I would be leaving empty handed," Charlie said.

Malcolm, sitting on the other side of the couch said, "Heck, I probably would leave with two dogs. And, I'm allergic. Dogs that work side-by-side saving our lives in combat shouldn't be treated as assets."

"Dad, did you say ass hat?" Ted joked, knowing full well he said 'asset.'

Mike's podcasts normally are conversational, hosting other veterans who tend to have published books sharing their own personal stories. The 'network of brotherhood' connected GTM with him through a friend of Malcolm's. Mike was far from being politically correct, and didn't care at all if the discussion became political. He joked about military wives being tougher than their husbands, and at one point during conversation, when GTM was becoming visibly angry over the CCSP bill, joked that maybe he should have had his own wife standing by as security.

It certainly was a first for Mike to host a homeschooling mom, never mind one with a doctorate in engineering. Nearly all his questions were about understanding the CCSP bill and GTM's ideas on different solutions.

GTM knew she found the right guy when at one point he said, "Do you think any of these $#!Theads in Congress even read this bill?"

Jake's eyes lit up on this. "Huh, Mom didn't smack him for saying a cuss word?"

"Don't worry little buddy, I am sure Mike's wife will smack him after, for your mom." Charlie glanced at Malcolm—the innocence of youth.

"I fell asleep twice reading this awful CCSP bill, prepping for this podcast. Can you believe the stuff they embedded in the 3,845 pages? Why would money for a rabies vaccination be budgeted in public education?"

Texas, like Florida, was also planning on becoming an early adopter of the program, and Mike had a vested interest, with two daughters in grade school. The fact that the bill forced the 90,000+ Florida homeschooled children and roughly 350,000+ Texas homeschooled children into public schools, went against every concept of freedom imaginable to him.

The interview ended, GTM said her goodbyes and headed for the airport for the trip home. Three hours later, back in Florida, waiting outside the secured area where his mom would appear after her plane landed, Jake was glued to Ted's phone, demonstrating videos of over-performing Malinois dogs. This breed was definitely back at that foundation's ranch.

This is the dog for me!

The Malinois, like Jake, exuded so much energy it is unable to sit still for any length of time.

The children couldn't wait to see what type of dog GTM would bring home. When she arrived empty handed, their spirits were completely crushed, to the point of barely greeting her. Each had their own special dog mentally picked out. Jake wanted an eager, over-ambitious, tons of energy Malinois. Ted would be grateful for a retired German Shepherd, who liked calm walks, lap space and hugs. And, Rosa was in love with the idea of an adorable Golden Retriever puppy.

Instead of a dog, GTM came back with a mission. She was going to stop all twelve states from becoming early adopters of CCSP. The podcast started an avalanche of people connecting with her, who actually wanted to discuss and understand CCSP. Their mom kept busy doing Skype interviews, speaking engagements and even creating rallies. For the first time she wasn't alone in her efforts, either. The protest group that initially was opposed to the CCSP bill when it was pushed through federally, jumped back into action. They stuck with the original black-and-white, prison-stripe theme that they wore back at Congressman Harris's speech in Washington. The only difference was that now news outlets actively sought them out. The press was always negative, but they held to the adage that 'even bad publicity is good publicity.'

Rosa couldn't understand it. "That statement doesn't make sense. If food critics give a restaurant bad reviews, it can put them out of business!"

Ted tried to explain, "Not being talked about is worse."

"But we are going to be talked about as the HOME-SCHOOLED FREAKS by EVERYONE. Mom is everywhere TALKING ABOUT US, even showing pictures of us." Rosa said, but she wasn't exaggerating.

GTM was EVERYWHERE. She connected with people, and started grass roots efforts, forming alliances with groups of petitioners in all twelve states, that were putting forth bills of their own CCSP version to become early adopters. The conversation was nationwide.

Prison stripes became a fad for all opposed to the CCSP bill, and people opposing the bill continued open dialogue under #ccspiskidnapping. Ted gloated often taking full credit for coining the hashtag.

He devised a Twitter campaign with summertime cell phone buddy Max Sweet, and the two even created anonymous Twitter accounts. Every day, Ted would tweet a fact contained in the CCSP bill. Max, even though he dreaded the idea of CCSP passing in New York, would pretend to be an antagonist and attack Ted's statement, claiming that it was a lie and worse. The two created all out Twitter wars. Both learned fast where the line was, before their account was suspended. They competed with each other on who could troll better and sucker the bigger celebrity or sports figure into the battle.

Ted learned how much more traction a Tweet would generate when it was accompanied by a picture. He didn't have the capability or know how, but he soon discovered fellow like-minded accounts, who would create awesome memes against CCSP for him. Often, he would Direct Message (DM) them, prior to his daily tweet of the day asking for assistance.

The prison stripe fad became dangerous. The essence of their messages was that "Brave people wear stripes." The messages drove home the point that stripe wearers were brave because there was always the chance of being attacked by an 'anti-igno' mob.

Anti-igno was a new term created and short for 'anti-ignorance.' Anti-Igno was the counter protest group made up primarily of university students in support of CCSP, which they argued was created to fight illiteracy and ignorance. Unfortunately, the #ccspiskidnapping numbers paled in comparison to the 'anti-igno' crowd. Anti-igno was practically an oxymoron, because its supporters were extremely uninformed. They never looked into the CCSP bill to understand or articulate their views, and flat-out refused speaking engagements, especially debates. They were known for wearing black, covering their faces, and when not wearing helmets while committing acts of vandalism and violence, would sport graduation caps. They always traveled in packs of six or more. You certainly didn't want to run into them alone while wearing stripes.

On Twitter, random accounts added stripes to their profile pictures, and they even formed Twitter follow trains, all under #CCSPISKIDNAPPING.

Meanwhile, in the Catskills, the Sweet children were secretly hoping their summertime friends would move next to them permanently to avoid CCSP, since it had yet to be pushed in New York.

They decided to create a ghost video on SSweet1776, and dedicate it to GTM. They titled it *The Hell of CCSP*. The four children convinced their mom to take them to visit Letchworth Village, which was an hour-and-a-half drive away. Little did they realize the place would be rotting out, with 'No Trespassing' signs posted everywhere.

Letchworth Village was originally modeled after Thomas Jefferson's estate in Monticello back in 1911, and sat on 2,362 acres. It should have been stunningly beautiful. The children had even dressed head to toe in prison-stripe costumes they found at the Salvation Army store.

Sam felt awful.

Every life has meaning! Geraldo Rivera released that old documentary, Willowbrook: The Last Great Disgrace years ago. With evidence like that, why wasn't this place closed down long before 1996. How can anyone neglect people like that? I can't believe Letchworth Village didn't become something else, anything else.

Standing outside the fence, surrounded by four sad faces looking at the dilapidated buildings set amongst falling autumn leaves, their mom mischievously asked, "Do you think your father's wire cutters are still in the trunk?"

The children stared at her in disbelief.

Looking back at the children, she said, a tad defensively, "If GTM can take on both political party sides of our government, the least I can do is help you children with a little trespassing!"

Max ran to the car. Sam, Cody and Scout asked what they could do next.

"Now don't go thinking your mom is cool with breaking rules. First, NEVER, EVER let me catch you doing something like this. Second, we have to stay safe and be overly careful. Third, try not to touch anything. And MOST important, the story to your father is that a nice old security guard was kind enough to walk us around. He knows I can talk people into doing almost anything!"

The children discovered that their mom had one heck of a hidden devious streak. She had Max park the car behind some bushes, a little-ways up the road. "That way, if it is spotted, it wouldn't be obvious as to why the car is here. We say we are out for an autumn walk, taking pictures of the leaves as part of a research project on tree dormancy." The next thing that took them off guard was her instructions on cutting a straight line in the wire fence, starting from the bottom going about three-feet high, in line with one of the fence posts. "Doing it that way will make it harder to notice."

Grey, overcast clouds made the setting of the buildings appear creepy, even at 3:00 p.m. Max started the video, focused on one specific big dark cloud in the sky, then scanned up the hill to the one that already was dormant, possibly dead tree amongst all the other beautiful fall maples that had just started to drop their yellow and red leaves.

Then, from about fifteen-feet away, he panned the phone over to Cody, standing on one of the massive broken windowsills. The setting showed the graffiti on the front of the institution with broken windows, busted doors, and half-rotting roof.

Cody started with basic facts, as Max walked closer with the phone, to ensure he picked up every word. Cody said, "Letchworth Village insane asylum was established in 1911, to help society by housing the community's mentally unstable, feeble-minded, and physically disabled children and adults. It was a government-run facility that did good for society by helping desperate people in need of twenty-four-seven care. The

Letchworth Village insane asylum had consisted of 130 buildings, and could support 3,000 patients. However, they were good at what they did, and by 1935, twenty-four years after they first opened their doors, they massively exceeded the 3,000-patient capacity."

Sam took over as a slight drizzle began. "Letchworth Village insane asylum exceeded its capacity in 1935, smack in the middle of the Great Depression, which ran from 1929 to 1939. This was at a time when even healthy, capable people were struggling to survive. Families were forced to abandon the sick and weak among their family. Many would even abandon newborns.

"Letchworth Village didn't turn anyone away! Some thought they were saints for doing so. The appearance of nurses assisting patients, walking them up these wide white steps and columned entrance to the main building, gave families peace of mind that they were doing the right thing. However, those families didn't see what was really going on.

"What they didn't want to ask themselves was how in the middle of the Great Depression can Letchworth Village afford to be this saving grace?"

The one dark cloud let loose cold rain, coming down hard, but the boys showed no sign of wanting to go inside that main building. It was CREEPY! Scout walked over, grabbed her mom's hand, saying "Girls are so much tougher than boys!" and walked inside without hesitation.

Max followed, phone in hand, telling Cody and Sam to stand guard and whistle if they saw anyone coming. In the main hallway, Scout smiled at her big brother and questioned, "Why do you always give them an out?"

Just then an old door fell to the floor, off an old, rusted hinge. Scout's gaze went straight to the room the door once shielded. "It's a sign. Let's go that way."

Max looked at his mother. "In for a penny, in for a pound" she said.

Max then answered Scout's question, "Same reason I always back you up on your stupid ideas!"

Scout wasn't listening though.

Inside the room were two rows of white, rusting, tiny metal bed frames crammed within one foot of each other, lining each wall. A few had the remains of mattresses on them, most revealed rusted metal springs.

"We film my part right here," Scout announced. Max complied. Scout stood dead center amid the two rows of tiny beds, which extended toward the rear of the endlessly long room, like railroad tracks disappearing in the distance. It looked horrifying!

She began, "In the middle of the Great Depression, Letchworth Village wasn't the saving grace families were trusting it to be. As you can see around me, massive numbers of children were placed here, not just mentally or physically handicapped children, but regular children whose families abandoned them. Letchworth Village never questioned or turned anyone away, especially children, even in the middle of the Great Depression!

"Instead they found a way to profit. Science needed experimental subjects, and lives didn't count at Letchworth Village. The most profitable activity was testing medications and vaccinations. It is rumored children would remain strapped into these beds for weeks, barely being fed. Who could eat anyway, with dead and dying bodies covered in their own filth, lying right next to you?

"Imagine the horror of abandoning your baby, in hopes to save it from starvation, then finding out that starving to death would have been considered kind and compassionate, in comparison to what really happened here!

"Besides being haunted, we chose Letchworth Village because CCSP is a bill that is eager to take your children away. Much like CCSP, Letchworth Village was intended to help communities, however, once established it was used to perpetrate evil...TRUE EVIL!"

For dramatics, Scout skipped away, with her right hand touching the end of each metal frame as she went down the row singing, "CCSP is kidnapping me, CCSP is kidnapping me!"

"Okay, scary enough! Let's go. Besides, the boys are still outside. They are probably drenched by now," insisted their mom.

As they were about to leave the room, Scout stopped and pointed towards an old medicine cabinet, tipped on its side, "Who is SHE?"

"Scout, not funny! I'm not as gullible as Sam or Cody," Max snapped.

"She wants us to open the cabinet." Scout said. Max looked at his mother. They both got chills.

"Nope we are leaving," her mother insisted, reaching for Scout's hand. It was too late. Scout's hand was grabbing the cabinet handle and turning it.

Scout had to yank hard to jar the cabinet door. The faintest whisper of a small siren-like shrill started and stopped.

"That sounds like a..." their mother paused, and then jumped into action, helping Scout with the cabinet door. "A KITTEN," she said, finishing her sentence.

The limp little body of a black-and-brown striped, slightly spotted kitten, lay there, barely able to open its eyes. It was all alone. The family guessed it had gotten trapped somehow in the cabinet, and the mother cat, unable to rescue it, just left it. Max wrapped it up in his sweatshirt for warmth, and they all rushed down to the car to see if they could get it to drink a little bottled water.

The entire trip home Max sat with the snug little creature smaller than a fist snuggled in his sweatshirt in his lap, clinging onto life as he slowly dipped his finger in the bottle and placed water droplets on the tiny kitten's tongue.

Their mother warned them, "Don't get attached, in case it doesn't survive."

"If it lives, can we call it Casper?" asked Scout.

"It isn't a white cat. How about Tiger?" commented Cody.

"How did you two manage to stay dry?" Mrs. Sweet asked.

"It stopped raining the minute you were inside" answered Cody. "It was freaky, as if the rain happened on purpose to make you go in," said Sam.

"It was on purpose." Scout said.

"No one can control the rain," said Sam.

"Kathleen can," replied Scout.

"Who is Kathleen?" asked Cody.

"Kathleen is the little girl that made the door fall, and got me to open the cabinet," answered Scout.

"Scout, there was no little girl," Max said.

"Yes! There was! She disappeared right when we found Casper. She wanted us to help it. She said it was abandoned just like her."

Everyone in the car went silent for a long time after that.

After they arrived home, Ted and Max doubled down on pushing the YouTube video. They titled it, The Hell of CCSP!!! They went back and added it as a comment tagged to every Twitter discussion chain with #CCSP #CCSPISKIDNAPPING they could find.

Max even created an Instagram account, posting photos from Letchworth Village and listed the video in the comments. It was the most viewed Ghost Story the channel had posted so far.

The fact that the Sweet children gained a cat while creating it, gave Rosa more ammunition to beg for a dog. Scout emailed them pictures. The kitten was adorable. It had little black points on the tips of its ears and a short tail about half the length of a normal cat. Mr. Sweet insisted on naming the kitten, Bob, only explaining that the children would soon understand.

After seeing The Hell of CCSP video, Rosa felt like a complete coward for not wearing stripes. Hoping to gain outside support, she asked Master John, "Doesn't wearing stripes go against the rule of avoid the fight at all costs if possible?"

"FUUU... FUDGE THEM!" Master John quickly recovered and rephrased his initial reaction. "You should feel open to wear whatever you want without fear of harm. Sorry for almost saying a bad word."

This wasn't the response Rosa was hoping to get. Sure, she supported her mom, but she didn't want the attention of wearing stripes.

In contrast, Ted and Jake lived in stripes. Rosa finally provided a false claim that she read online horizontal stripes make a person appear fat.

"Rosa, you are going to be at more risk wearing rainbows at school than stripes any day of the week," Ted said.

"What? Why?" she asked.

"Look, you have to be who you are and hold firm to it, without being intimidated," Ted exclaimed. "At public school, kids will pick on you for anything and everything. Remember what Jiu Jitsu is teaching us—stand up for yourself and be strong in your convictions. The bully will find someone weaker to target."

Ted realized his emotions were reflecting in how loud he was talking at that moment. He couldn't help it. He hated the idea of Jake and Rosa getting picked on. He even realized and regretted that he was a bit of a bully back in Miami. Maybe that was why no one stayed in touch with him after he moved. Perhaps they didn't miss him, maybe they weren't really friends.

Meanwhile, Courtney, the thug from the bookstore, became the face of the 'anti-igno' coalition. Tampa police were able to identify Courtney shortly after Isabella released an edited video from the bookstore.

Fellow university students reported on Courtney, for the mere $100 dollar reward. The viral video emphasized GTM clenching the girl's arm, practically rabid looking in appearance.

Rosa quickly asked Ted, "Will the children at school pick on us over this video, too?"

Ted hesitated, then he just nodded.

I can deal with wearing something besides rainbows or stripes so I don't get picked on, but there is no outliving everyone seeing Mom attacking some college girl.

The video was edited perfectly. It cut off prior to Courtney screaming, "You're going to die now!"

The bookstore publicly announced GTM was banned nationwide on any of their premises. The coffee shop one-upped them, creating a massive campaign in support of young people "who care" like Courtney.

They mass produced 'Courtney Cups,' depicting the outline of a rebellious girl's face with gouged ears, wearing a face mask in the form of a heart. There was public debate on whether Courtney should even be convicted of vandalism. Sure, she did it, and vandalism was bad, but she vandalized for the right reasons. Courtney was ultimately found guilty, but only penalized with mandatory community service. The true insult was when a GoFundMe account was formed, netting Courtney $428,733 in the first two weeks it was established.

Nonetheless, all of GTM's efforts almost worked. The bill may have passed federally by distraction and misdirection, but on the local state level it was heavily voted down. Of the twelve states that put it forward, only three adopted it, and those three passed it on extremely narrow margins. What confused GTM the most was that bigger government bureaucracies, especially in education, were usually a Democratic push. All twelve states tended to be Republican leaning, and like Florida, which had high ranking Republicans like Congressman Harris championing the bill.

GTM and Charlie were discussing the anomaly when Rosa raised her voice, "Mom! Your mission is over! Can we please stop talking about CCSP and go back to being normal?"

Rosa stomped out of the kitchen. Charlie was about to go after her when GTM stopped him. "She is really scared about going to public school."

Charlie looked over to Jake, "How about you? Aren't you scared?" Looking up from the smiley face he made in his mashed potatoes, Jake answered, "No way. Ted and I have been practicing some moves slightly altering Master John's lessons. Kids will regret it if they pick on me!"

Jake saying that, made GTM think of her own personal bully, Congressman Harris's aide Isabella. What was it again, 'Get louder and it gets worse?' GTM was not only loud, she was effective. Unfortunately, not effective enough to stop CCSP in Florida, but nine other states stopped it. The other two states passing CCSP were Texas and Georgia.

When instant retaliation didn't happen, GTM prayed.

Maybe the Congressman's aide, Isabella, doesn't have the ability. Perhaps with Florida's passing CCSP, she felt victorious and let go thoughts of revenge.

I know one thing for certain, I couldn't live with myself if I didn't try to stop this bill. All my instincts tell me something is really wrong about this bill.

What would happen if Isabella's retaliation targeted the children? I can accept any consequences that extend to me, but retaliation against the children would be a different issue.

14

WHEN NOTHING GOES RIGHT, GO LEFT!

CCSP had passed.

While the passage of the bill devastated most of the 'platoon,' Rosa, on the other hand, declared, "MISSION OVER!"

For German Tiger Mom, the mission was far from over.

So long as I can breathe, I am going to fight this! However, for now, I will put it aside to take full advantage of the little time left before the children are forced into public school. Besides, I have to meet with administrators to arrange the best placement for each of the children.

"But they are entering school in January, halfway through a school year..." was the canned excuse every administrator at

Robinson High School repeated to GTM, on EVERY request she had for proper placement of the children.

Gosh did they rehearse?

In fact, every single administrator and teacher used the same logic.

The twins qualified to be three grade levels higher academically than their age group. Ted, although he hadn't been home-schooled long, qualified academically one grade higher.

The State registered the children at Robinson High School, based on their zip code. GTM loved the mile away distance from their home, but the school didn't rank well. The school had begun implementing advanced technical learning curricula a few years earlier. Two contrasting school programs functioned in the one building. Part of the school focused on advanced learning; the other part pushed students along for the sake of graduating them. Funding dollars were tied to graduation rates, so if a few F or D grades were embellished to help pass students along, roll with it, better to prevent drop-out numbers.

GTM sat down with advisers who planned on placing the twins two grade levels beyond their age, as freshmen with the general student body. This would make them twelve-year-olds sitting among fourteen-year-olds, just entering high school, but academically more advanced. That dynamic spelled disaster for the children. GTM didn't even like the idea of Ted being advanced into the tenth grade with older students, although she knew no one would dare pick on him.

No matter how much GTM tried to get the children in the advanced learning classes, even if she had to keep them back learning at their own age level, she was shot down. "It is halfway through the school year! Those programs are full!"

Hmm, an internal memo must have been sent forcing teach-ers to repeat that exact statement across the State to every homeschooled parent.

Visibly upset after visiting Robinson High School, GTM drove to Gracie Tampa South MMA hoping for a few moments of quiet, to just observe the children at the dojo and watch them train. Lucky for her, only one other parent observed training that day, and the woman tended to avoid her.

Somehow the sight of Ted, Jake, and Rosa training, being typical children, calmed her.

They are far from eighteen, but these three are becoming strong-willed, good-hearted people. Even though they have much to learn, I am certain the world will be a better place, be-cause they exist.

Mike, a fellow thirteen-year-old Jiu Jitsu student, had reg-istered to participate in a North American Grappling Associa-tion—or NAGA as it was referred to—tournament, scheduled for November 23rd in Kissimmee, Florida. As Master John handed GTM the flier encouraging fellow students to attend for moral support, Jake snatched it.

Master John explained to Jake, "Master Matt requires that before anyone can compete, representing the dojo, that per-son, child or adult, must pass a rigorous test to be selected as part of the competition team. You three children are not yet ready to qualify for the team, so tournaments are not an op-tion. The flier is intended to encourage fellow students to at-tend and observe."

GTM hid her relief, since registering to compete would have cost $85.00 per child, never mind ancillary fees that go along with the registration fee.

Charlie and I are going to have to budget for back to school expenses. Meanwhile, goal planning to qualify on the competi-

tion team is free and an ideal distraction for the children versus their recent idée fixé on public school life.

Master John clapped his hands and said, "Let's get a few rolls in." With that he set the electronic timer to seven minutes, and continued, "All right kids! Find a partner to pair up with, and for the love of God go easy on each other! Remember this is only practice and be thankful for your training partners."

Jake looked around anxious. Every other child had been rolling for at least a year. Jake, wanting to go with what he knew, looked to partner up with Rosa or Ted. Mike, being right there, asked him if he wanted to roll.

I can't say no, but Mike is the best in the class.

Master John approached Mike. "Since you are going to the competition let's work on your bottom game. Mike start down. Jake try to pass his guard."

With that Master John commanded, "Shake hands, and again, I said go easy!" With that, the electronic timer gave three high pitched chimes.

Mike began in a butterfly guard sitting on his butt with his heels drawn inward. Jake approached Mike trying to step between his legs. Mike quickly scooted forward grabbing Jake's right arm with his left hand simultaneously grabbing at the back of Jake's head with his right arm. As Mike switched his feet—bringing his left heel back closer to his butt—and extending his right leg behind Jake's knee, Jake knew instantly Mike was going for an elevator sweep.

Jake quickly did a wet dog—shifting his head side to side as a dog would to rid itself of excess water. Because of doing a wet dog, Mike was unable to control Jake's head. Jake quickly grabbed Mike's right wrist and shot his other hand behind Mike's right triceps, in almost a handshakes grip.

As Jake pulled Mike towards him, he moved fast and pulled himself around to take Mike's back. Jake became instantly grateful that Ted tried this move on him all the time. As he began to take Mike's back, Master John shouted, "Hooks and harness, hooks and harness!" As Jake locked in a seatbelt grip and got his grips in, he brought Mike to the under-hook side.

Mike grabbed Jake's choke arm with both hands, preventing Jake from sinking in the rear naked choke. Jake kept trying to break Mike's grip, but every time he did Mike just re-gripped. Jake was in a stalemate. In a competition, this would cost Mike points, but in practice it didn't do either of them any good. Ted just muscled through these, but that wouldn't work for Jake.

Master John yelled, "If it's not working move on."

Jake began to roll Mike towards his choke arm, but as Mike started to clear Jake's hooks, Jake threw his right leg over Mike's right shoulder, bringing him back to the side they were just on. Again, Mike went after the choke arm, but this time Jake pushed his head away. Jake brought his leg up and over Mike's head, setting up for the arm bar. Isolating Mike's left arm, Jake used his weight against Mike and locked in the arm bar.

Master John yelled, "Fast in the transitions, slow with the submissions." Jake extended Mike's arm by leaning back until he felt a tap on his leg. Master John quickly announced, "TAP! Let him go, Jake."

Holy cow! Did that really happen? No way! I actually got someone to tap, not just someone—MIKE.

Jake jumped up and exclaimed, "WOOWHOOO! It worked! I can't believe it worked!"

Just then, the electronic timer made its three chimes and the roll ended. "Nice job guys. Shake hands with your partners and line up on the wall," Master John said, while Jake still celebrated.

Master John gave Jake 'the look.' Jake quieted right down and took his place with the others on the wall, from left to right lowest belts to the highest belts. He lined up on one end, Mike the other.

Did that really just happen?

Jake tried to hide the glow on his face, and couldn't.

GTM whispered to Mike's mom, "Did Mike allow Jake a false victory?"

Abbey admitted, "I don't know. If he did, he didn't warn me about it."

Being the only mothers observing class that day, the woman had almost no choice but to chit chat with GTM.

Abbey and her husband met as high school sweethearts, and she helped support him through college, and then they took a bigger risk together when they started a consulting firm together. The consulting firm became a success and although an acquisition 'muddled the waters.' He encouraged her not to work, which gave her plenty of time to observe Mike's Jiu Jitsu practice.

Abbey heard about the chaos GTM and the children went through. She knew only what the news reported.

"I imagine I only know a fraction of the real story. To confess, Mike is good friends with Hunter Harris. I would say 'best friends,' but Plant High School doesn't permit use of the term 'best friend,' out of its no bullying policy. The fear is that anyone without a 'best friend' will have hurt feelings."

"Hunter's parents are real pieces of work. I feel bad for the child. I even tried to convince his mother to let Hunter vacation with our family during the summer on a Mediterranean Cruise, but Megan, Hunter's Mom, didn't return any of my calls or voicemails. I regret not trying harder. Hunter seemed different after spending the summer touring with Congressman Harris. Mike's good and I trust him to be good, but I am grateful he has been learning Jiu Jitsu, in case Hunter's new-found personality lands them in the wrong kind of trouble."

"I have to politely disagree with you Abbey. Whatever goodness you thought Hunter had, no longer can possibly exist."

GTM then pulled up the SSweet1776 channel on her phone, logged in and showed how horrible Hunter acted when they met him at The Bogota. The full private video showed Hunter's rant and included the part where Hunter hit Rosa in the face.

"So, you signed the children up for Jiu Jitsu all for Rosa? I'm just asking because she doesn't seem to like it that much," commented Abbey.

"Gosh no, if I was going to sign the children up for something based on Rosa, we would be in a cooking class. And not an ordinary class, a Gordon Ramsey chef level class—I imagine preparing something like Beef Wellington!" Both women laughed at that.

Abbey confessed, "I hate the idea of CCSP. Mike is my only child, and although he attends public school, I love being a stay-at-home mom. Mike means everything to me, maybe more than Chip, my husband, even!"

Laughing Abbey continued, "I often embarrass Mike by bringing him homemade lunches in front of his classmates. Nothing as fancy as Beef Wellington, but homemade, nonetheless. Each day, when he comes home, we sit down and review what he learned. This way I can add perspective to his lessons. I even hire a tutor to help him learn anything that is beyond me—for example, when his French grade slipped to a B. My southern drawl didn't lend itself to helping in the slightest. Come January I am going to be totally lost."

"Hey, maybe we should take up a painting or cooking class together, since Rosa is most likely more skilled in the kitchen than both of us," Abbey said.

GTM appreciated the act of friendship, but admitted, "I am already exploring what is required to become a certified teacher and get the children back to being homeschooled."

Abbey, still stuck on the topic of food, had another suggestion.

"H.B. Plant high school has a phenomenal student nutrition program that children help and participate in. If Rosa enjoys cooking, she would love it. Besides, another anti-bullying policy Plant has will prevent Rosa from being beat up for wearing rainbows."

GTM smiled and responded, "That would be a great thing! For the first time in his life Jake has caught up to Rosa in size, and I am trying to prevent it, but he has twelve years of payback built up. Rosa always pushed him around! Now, for some strange reason she believes that rainbows help her be stronger than Jake, so I am not sure she will ever stop wearing them."

Wow, Paco is right! Jiu Jitsu is a great fit for the children. It's already helping them to gain confidence, and become more well-rounded. It also just helped me connect with Abbey.

Abbey seemed so excited by her own idea, she all but guaranteed she could get the children enrolled at H.B. Plant high school. Abbey continued informing GTM about the school. "It is only four miles from Robinson High, but is completely different.

"The school's enrollment is roughly 2,500 students, which is about 1,000 more than Robinson, but the curriculum is more advanced, and the school has smaller classroom sizes. It is the best school around, public or private.

"The students there are extremely competitive, academically and athletically. Administers pride themselves each year, not only on the fact that everyone graduated, but on how many graduates are accepted into Ivy League colleges.

GTM researched the school later that day and found the information so interesting that she spoke to the computer to think it though.

"Henry B. Plant is located in the prestigious Palma Ceia area zip code. There is even a prestigious 'Palma Ceia Country Club' as part of the exclusive zip code! Wow, it's apparent what kind of children attend this school, that zip includes some of those side roads that have hidden mansions on them. I'm sure the children will never be approved to attend here. There's no hurt in letting Abbey try anyway.

"Plant High is roughly three miles more from our residence. Robinson's one-mile distance is more ideal, but Plant seems better in all other aspects. If CCSP is true to honoring school choice, enrolling the children at Plant should be okay.

"Rosa would love participating in a nutrition program. Ah, I better wait to tell her. With Congressman Harris's Assistant being out for blood, the last thing we will get is approval to attend the same school as his son! If the worst happens and we are denied enrollment, it can be one more piece of evidence I can use to support my right to homeschool."

Abbey even offered to arrange and meet with administrators on her behalf, claiming she had endless influence at the school. They dare not turn the children down without hearing her out. Abbey accredited her influence to countless hours of chaperoning and fundraising which may matter for something for once.

Early morning, a day after her conversation with Abbey, GTM's phone buzzed with an incoming call from an unrecognized number. The number had a Tallahassee area code.

The State of Florida could never review and approve the children's enrollment paperwork that fast, they must be denying the children's entrance to Plant.

She answered the phone ready to argue, the exact opposite news graced her ears. The children were all accepted into Plant. GTM decided on a day of celebration. The dedication of the ghost video from the Sweet children gave her the idea to experiment and start the day with her own attempt at ghost story telling.

"The Tampa courthouse building is now a hotel known as Amicus Curiae. The courthouse turned 108 years old in 2013, when renovated, and it was very much in need of renovations. Up until that time, if you were a public citizen serving on a jury, you still had your choice of bathrooms."

"You mean girls, boys and family Mom, or the new transgender neutral bathrooms?" Rosa asked.

"Wait, what?" GTM stepped back in surprise. "Where did you learn about transgender neutral bathrooms?" She asked.

"Piper, from Jiu Jitsu class mentioned it. She said rainbows reflect a community of people confused if they are girls or boys. There are girls who like other girls, boys who like other boys, girls who wish they were boys, and boys who wish they were girls. It's a good thing, more people wearing rainbows. They are kryptonite over Jake."

GTM smiled.

Pride Parades will forever symbolize Rosa being happy that more people wear rainbows.

"Wearing rainbows is a good thing Rosa, but all the options you mentioned are people exercising freedom of choice, which is why this country is great. We have freedom. People should never have to, but their sexual preference can be hidden. The difference in the courthouse bathrooms existed from the time of segregation and days of slavery. You can't hide your skin color. Until remodeled, the courthouse had real nice bathrooms, or not so nice bathrooms of the same sex only about twenty feet apart. The south was stupid and stayed heavily segregated for so long. Segregation wouldn't allow black people and white people together."

Ted jumped in on the conversation. "Southerners were almost all Democrats, and used to lynch black folks, as well as white Republicans, long after the Civil War ended. Andrew Johnson, a Democrat from Tennessee, who took office after Lincoln was assassinated, undid so much of the good Lincoln accomplished in the Civil War. He got rid of protection for former slaves. Lincoln only picked Johnson as a running mate for political purposes, to help show solidarity between the North and South. He didn't like the man at all. Do you know the first gun restriction laws were established to disarm black folks so they couldn't protect themselves from the Ku Klux Klan?"

"Ted, you are doing a lot of side studying," GTM said.

"I know and it isn't the happiest of subjects, but I had to. Deep down I have this strange feeling I have been lied to. I realize in school only so much can get discussed, but this is important stuff, and I don't understand why the school didn't cover it. We did cover the Three-Fifths Compromise, but so vaguely I thought it meant a black person didn't count as much as a white person. I didn't realize it was enacted to prevent slave owners from getting too much representation in Congress. Guess I should have been paying better attention."

GTM countered with, "That's okay. You already learned the most important lesson— 'never stop learning.' I still have A LOT to learn about telling ghosts stories, because the ghost that haunts Amicus Curiae, otherwise known as the old courthouse, is Charlie Wall. Not a black man, an evil organized crime boss from the 1950s.

"Charlie Wall mysteriously wound up dead when he planned to 'tell all.' Rosa, the part you will like is Amicus Curiae now has a fancy restaurant called Bethel's Brewhouse in it. The hotel also partners with the Tampa Museum of Art.

Would you children enjoy a day of filming a ghost video, eating a fancy lunch and going to the museum after for a change?"

Rosa stared downward at her feet. GTM wondered if she should tell the children the good news about acceptance at Plant High School now, or wait until the restaurant.

Jake spoke up, "Mom, can we park at the Fort Brooke Parking Garage if we go? It is only a couple blocks away from it."

"Sure, Jake. Does it matter where we park, though?" asked GTM.

Pulsing his hands out in front of him and lowering his voice Jake said, "In 1980, while excavating the Fort Brooke Parking Garage to ensure its foundation, bones were unearthed—HUMAN BONES—LOTS OF HUMAN BONES."

Jake stood up from the kitchen table and began pacing as he spoke. "At first they thought the bones belonged to Native American tribes. Seminole Indians once populated the area. It was then realized that the area was an old cemetery for soldiers. Perhaps soldiers from the Embalmed Beef Scandal. No one is sure. They could even have been older than that and belonged to Conquistadors.

"The discovery was viewed by all as a mere inconvenience! No one dared to pay money to test the bones forensically, because discovering the truth about the bones would have prevented continuation of the much-needed parking garage."

Jake paused, for dramatics. "The building of the garage continuuuued!"

Jake stared at all of them. Even GTM was locked in, wanting to hear more. "People who build garages do so as cheap as possible. The builders didn't have to worry about resale value being impacted because people don't live in garages. The local newspaper published an article about elaborate excavation teams removing all those bones and transferring them to a sanctuary, but it was a hoax. A hoax all made up to continue and get permits approved.

"People who build garages are often 'connected' if you know what I mean." Jake pushed his fingers against his nose to indicate a broken nose. "For all we know it could be Charlie Wall getting revenge on a shady business deal. What we do know for sure, is there is no sanctuary, no documentation, no excavation teams either.

"What is fact is that the men contracted to work on the garage would suddenly quit, NEVER TO BE SEEN AGAIN! They wouldn't even return to collect their final paychecks. This wasn't limited to common workers Lead foremen also disappeared. It is said that the Fort Brooke poltergeists, yes plural, haunted the men until they quit, went crazy or died. It took ages to complete the garage."

"Jake, construction workers can be women. Why do you have to be such an attention hog? 'Look at me. I'm Jake, I'm awesome in Jiu Jitsu, and I can tell killer ghost stories!' Rosa huffed. "Mom, I don't want to go if Congressman Harris the Horrible is speaking again?"

Ah, the real reason Rosa isn't excited!

GTM said, "Rosa, this one is really only for us. In fact, I have some good news specifically for you that you will want to hear. I am sorry your Bogota experience was so terrible! Although there is one change of plans. We will take your father's SUV, after Jake's story! There is no way I am going to risk getting a poltergeist in my car! Why on earth wouldn't anyone halt construction after a discovery like that? Awful!"

15

CARPE NOCTEM ORIGIN

It was the oddest Sunday night. Rosa pointed to the moon. An orange Cheshire smile glistened back through the Spanish moss hanging off the oak trees. At 9:00 p.m. the three children who had been waiting since 8:00 p.m., were running out of things to discuss with German Tiger Mom, who was standing by holding back her tears.

"How come you aren't this sad when Dad and Malcolm get deployed? They're going off to war, we are just going to school?" Jake asked.

"I am. I usually do a better job of hiding it," GTM lied.

Truth was, she trusted Charlie and Malcolm as forces to be reckoned with. Her children were still innocent children that could be used, manipulated and exploited. She hated everything about the world at that very moment. The news anchors who were quick to report a lie no matter who it hurt. The politicians who wielded influence for their own personal grasp at power. Big corporations who do the wrong things for a few extra pennies of profit. And, the worst, the part of the population who were so easy to manipulate.

For the first time ever, I am questioning my choice to be a stay-at-home mom.

Had I stayed on my career path as an engineer, Charlie and I would be considered one-percenters, with Jake and Rosa attending the finest boarding schools.

Just then, three A-10 Warthogs cut through the night, heading upwind off MacDill's runway four. They split across the view as if they were slapping the Cheshire smile of the moon. January, the beginning of a new budget year. GTM stared at them. It helped distract from her tears.

'Use it or lose it' funds, either being spent on JP4 fuel, or were the Warthogs being deployed to help troops with ground support in the ongoing wars that haven't been in the headlines in ages? Perhaps those Miss Universe contestants had it right —'World Peace'—the perfect unrealistic answer to all which is evil. I always envisioned giving the contestants who said it swirlies.

The bus pulled up. It was the most basic, old yellow standard school bus.

These things haven't changed in centuries!

The children boarded, having long been out-hugged and out-kissed by GTM.

Ted whispered, "To the back, the further back the better." Jake followed his lead.

Rosa scampering to catch up said, "Wait!" It was too late. The boys already sat down two rows from the back exit.

Ted whispered, "The cooler you are, the further back in the bus you sit. The further back in the bus, the more you can get away with."

"What are we getting away with?" Jake asked, excited.

"Shhhh. Nothing. It's all about perception. Act cool!" Ted said, as he took up the entire row behind them.

Rosa said, "Looking cool and smelling cool are apparently very different."

The odor was a mixture from fresh blue vinyl, dry dirt, and cheap metal.

"How do I turn off my nose?" Rosa complained. "Ted the back of the bus smells like a dirty footlocker."

Rosa looked at Jake. Jake shrugged his shoulders.

Copying Ted, Jake took out his new 'required' phone and pulled up Jiu Jitsu videos. Rosa, feeling left out, did the same, but pulled up the band, Skillet.

Thank goodness for headsets. Christian Pop isn't 'back of the bus type cool.'

Looking around, Rosa realized most children looked as confused as they were, except the other kids already knew each other. The other difference she picked up on was the fancy square roller board luggage bags and brand name new clothes. She and Jake had their shop-at -Walmart-much-clothes—according to Hunter—and Dad's left-over camouflage duffel bags, which were bursting at the seams to hold what each child required—two school uniforms, one set of pajamas, gym clothes and five sets of clean underwear.

GTM couldn't afford to buy new clothes or roller board luggage bags for the children, another thing sure to get them picked on. The school funding cards were tied to Robinson High School for the children. This made them invalid. She had no choice but to use the family credit card for the never-ending list of school essentials. Leaving her no other option, except to pay out of her pocket and deal with the State of Florida to process paperwork for reimbursement.

Casual attire was only permitted on the bus ride to school Sunday night, and Friday, which included the bus ride home.

In addition, each child had to have the required learning utensils in the new mandated, see-through bulletproof backpacks.

Education is a massive money laundering market. Notorious gangsters, like Tampa's late Charlie Wall, had nothing on todays' back-store handshakes.

The phones alone cost twice that of a new iPhone and were already old technology.

People with greasy palms are definitely getting rich somewhere.

As Rosa turned off the track after the third play through, she realized, looking out the bus window, that it was pulling up to Robinson High School!

All the children were exiting the bus towards the auditorium. Since the children were last to exit the bus, Rosa had to interrupt what appeared to be a full-fledged gossip circle to get the teachers' attention.

"What do you want?" snarled one of the teachers.

Rosa almost backed away, but Ted, grabbing Rosa's duffel bag out of her hand, said, "My sister wants to know why we are at Robinson High School, not Plant."

To his chagrin, a different teacher turned, putting her hands on her hips and chastised the two children for not paying attention. After which the snarling teacher spoke again. "I recognize you now. Aren't you that obnoxious woman's children?"

Rosa's teeth clenched in anger. Another, kindlier teacher stepped in front of the two women, extending her arm to lead the children back with the others.

"For now, Plant High School is to overnight at Robinson, because the air conditioning unit needs repair. You are all in the right spot."

Being in the back of the bus, last to enter the auditorium, Jake, Rosa and Ted got stuck with the last remaining two bunk beds by the auditorium doors.

"Woo-whoo! We got to stay up past midnight, and it isn't even New Years!" Jake bragged as he looked at the clock right above his head over the doors.

A resident assistant led the children to the locker room of their preferred gender, alphabetically by last name, to change into PJs. It was almost 2:00 a.m. when they settled in.

For what seemed like the five-hundredth time they heard a loud CLICK-CLICK sound that died away to a quieter click-click as another child got up to use the restroom. Ted realized the auditorium doors were inanimate objects, but he visualized them laughing at him. Ted tossed, facing away from the doors. He didn't know what was worse, the clicking noise or the strobe effect from the lit-up hallway.

Even prisoners were sectioned off two to a room. Plant's Junior High, which included seventh, eighth, and ninth graders were the only grades sent to Robinson, but Ted still figured there must be well over 1,000 students.

This is pure insanity!

By rolling over, Ted found himself staring face-to-face with Jake who was hanging upside down off the top bunk. Jake whispered, "I know something we can get away with! Whatever we do, let's keep these beds, they are the best for it."

Ted, before pulling the covers over his head answered, "Fine, but only if you start brushing your teeth more. Dang, did GTM make sauerkraut for dinner?"

Rosa, overhearing every word, answered, "Yes, with Boar's Head bratwurst sausages. She let me do the grilling. I even toasted the sesame rolls on the grill. They go better than poppy seed. It is like a German version of an American Sloppy Joe, or an Italian meatball hoagie. They were delicious! What are we getting away with? Whisper it to me."

Jake leaned over across the top bunks to Rosa, cupped his hand to her ear, and whispered, "I figured out how we can still get Jiu Jitsu practice in! We have to wait a few days though."

Jiu Jitsu?

Rosa was a little let down, but getting away with something sounded fun, so she answered, "Count me in! Ted was right about your brushing." Rosa pulled the cover up over her face, copying Ted's example.

The children woke to band cymbals being clanged by a pointy nosed child, roughly a year older than Ted. He then went on to dictate through a megaphone. "The routine every day is to follow the same format as the night. We do this in alphabetical order, based on last name. For those of you TOO STUPID to understand, when the letter of your last name is called, enter the locker room of your preferred gender to change into school uniforms."

This cymbal banging rat-face thinks he is boss.

"Who is the twit?" asked Ted, but no one responded.

The children decided it couldn't hurt to go along with the routine for now.

Rosa felt out of place when she realized that most of the thirteen-year-old girls, and all of the fourteen-year-olds, were wearing bras. Hoping for isolation, she walked towards the back of the locker room, only to encounter two very awkward boys. She decided to change her top in a stall when she peed.

Wow, is my body different than the other girls! These girls look almost grown up. Some even fuss with makeup.

"The lockers are for the Robinson students only!"

That's good, at least now I can hide when I change and no one will notice, expecting me to change in front of a specific locker.

Rosa would have smiled hearing that, if it wasn't said blaring right in her ear through a megaphone as she exited her 'preferred' locker room, by pointy-nose, no chin, rat face.

Returning to her cot before Jake came back, she said, "Ted. We should call the twit Willard!"

She forgot that she was in such close quarters. A half-dozen surrounding children laughed, and a boy four cots away, still trying to sleep, decided to shout, "Hey, WILLARD! SUCK ON IT! The megaphone, GO SUCK ON IT, WILLARD!"

This had a good portion of the auditorium laughing.

"Rosa, I thought I had to worry about your getting bullied, not becoming a bully," Ted said, smiling ear to ear. "Willard is a fitting name though, and he is asking for it. Okay, you can be mean to Willard, but only Willard!"

"Leave your luggage on your cots, and only take your book bags with you to the buses." Willard was relentless with the megaphone.

"Students are assigned specific buses on the morning trip only. The bus ride will take the place of homeroom. It is based on the FIRST LETTER OF YOUR LAST NAME!"

"Willard is intolerable!" Ted said.

"You will ride the bus aligned with your homeroom class during transport to Plant High School. Homeroom and roll call will take place on the bus to save time for your teacher. After the last class, you children are to regroup on any available bus, to be driven back to Robinson High School. Buses run from

3:30 p.m. to 4:30 p.m. this week and are extended to 5:30 p.m. next week for extracurricular activities," Willard continued.

"So much for being on a bus only twice a week!" Ted said. "Why is Willard saying 'you children'? I doubt he's any older than us."

The homeroom class the twins were directed to was on Bus 2. Being redirected from Bus 1 allowed Rosa to snag a seat three rows back.

Please, oh please, let me have a bus seat with a working window? Bus smell in the morning will make me vomit!

Just as Rosa snapped down the window to feel a slight breeze, a booming voice yelled, "YOUR NAME IS MURPHY! DO YOU REALLY THINK MMMMmm SITS NEXT TO G? WELLL-LLL, I'M WAITING?"

Rosa turned, and froze at the sight. A massively tall man, wearing an old-fashioned grey tweed cap, with the front part pulled down extra low to his eyebrows, stood leaning over her. His left arm extending out straight, covering the distance of an entire bus row as he pointed to the back.

Jake, two rows from the back of the bus, waved at Rosa to join him.

Rosa crouched down to squeeze out of the bench. While she passed the massive huffing man, ducking under his tree trunk of an arm, still waiting for his answer, she couldn't help observe, "Did you have onion bagel with lox for breakfast?"

To this, the man flushed an angry red. "NOW!" he shouted.

Rosa climbed over seats and children to get back by Jake. Jake, laughing, whispered, "You can have the window seat, but I'm not sure at the good it will do you. I don't think it works. Nikki in the bed under you warned me about him this morning. Sorry, I didn't mention it. I thought for sure you would just sit right next to me. Nikki's last name also begins with M. She had him for Homeroom and Biology last year. His name is Professor Luger. He alrcady memorized all our names and our faces.

"Professor Luger is the only teacher that doesn't have to call our names to do roll call. Other than Homeroom, he teaches science classes. Don't address him as mister or teacher or anything different than Professor Luger. He's a retired drill sergeant, pissed off at the world that he has to work instead of retiring. If it makes you feel better, Nikki said rumor has it his ex-wife took everything in an ugly divorce, and also gets half of his military pension."

"I can see why someone would divorce him. What's beyond me is how did someone ever marry him in the first place?" Rosa wondered out loud at Jake, as she tried opening the window, having zero luck.

It was 10:00 a.m. before the twins saw their first teacher standing at a blackboard. The class was Contemporary Social Issues. It was listed as a history course, and from the description GTM had, the impression was American History focused around the Civil War.

Jake whispered to Rosa, "Mom would have had us finishing Math, English and History already. This is going to be sooo easy. I wonder if their science experiments will at least be cool?"

"STAND UP" shouted Ms. Fischer. "WHOEVER SPOKE, STAND UP!"

Jake froze. All he did was whisper to his sister why was this woman yelling. Maybe someone else was speaking and he didn't notice. Jake looked around—all eyes were on him.

"I may be going blind, but I hear EVERYTHING!" The teacher then grabbed the front of Rosa's desk, sneering at Rosa and demanded, "You were talking, weren't you?"

"No, I ...," Rosa was interrupted by the teacher.

"Of course, it wasn't you, you're a girl. Who spoke to you?"

"I did," said Hunter, sitting near the back of class.

"No, I did" retorted Mike from a few seats in front of him.

Rosa and Jake turned around not realizing Hunter Harris was sitting in the same class.

Jake blurted out, "Hunter. You jerk!"

"That's the voice! You have detention. What's your name?" Ms. Fischer snarled.

Laughing, Hunter said, "His name is Jake Murphy, and he was talking to his queer brother Rosa." All the children laughed at Hunter's remark.

Rosa couldn't slouch lower in her seat.

Ms. Fischer didn't seem to care, "Both of you Jake, Rosa detention! Now not a word more from anyone."

As they left the room, Hunter surrounded by his friends, glared shaking his head at Jake. "Idiots."

Rosa grabbed Jake's arm, "He's not worth it."

It was their first official class of the day and the only one Jake and Rosa shared. They weren't aware, however, the minute Ms. Fischer logged them into the school app for detention, each received five demerits which counted against them in an overall school spirit score. The app's ingenious name was 3S representing School Spirit Score. Unlike being homeschooled, public school allowed so many variables to influence the children's curriculum.

Rosa's elected classes included French Level One, Environmental Science and a Visual Arts course.

All three can help me with cooking. French will help me when I travel abroad studying cooking in Paris. Environmental Science is a prerequisite for Chemistry of Food. There is no hiding this one from Mom, with the main text book titled, 'Real Maple Syrup.' Visual Arts may help me with the aesthetics to plating, although that is a stretch, but at least it fits my schedule well.

Jake took the opposite approach and picked subjects he already learned or thought would be fun for his electoral choices. They were Robotics, United States History and Cryptozoology.

The children were all mixed up with suggested grade levels on their electives. Rosa realized this as she sat surrounded by seventeen-year-olds in Visual Arts.

Jake thought his biggest issue was making it from one class to another. Algebra was going to be the longest hike since it was clear across the entire school campus from Cryptozoology.

Robotics class, which Jake was able to make in plenty of time, became an instant nightmare.

Upon entry, the teacher, Miss. D'Alesandro, called him up in front of everyone without allowing him to claim a seat. "Class, now class, we have a new student, Jake Murphy. Jake and his twin sister Rosa are new to our school. Please welcome Jake? Jake, please tell us why you are interested in robotics?"

Jake shifted as he stood in front of an entire classroom full of kids older than him. "Well, I thought…"

"Jake, we don't actually care. What we do care about is why your mommy feels public educators are so scary she went as far as to track a college girl down in a bookstore and break her arm? No need responding, take a seat. Oh look, the only one left is center front. Right where I can keep my eyes on you!"

Rosa was amazed by how much time was spent worrying where to be and at what time, making it back to her locker between classes, only to switch books and run to her next class, all in effort hoping not to be late or singled out for any reason.

The nutrition program for that first week was already planned, but she was told on Wednesday that anyone wanting to participate should meet after school in the cafeteria.

I can't wait to tell Jake about this. Wait, oh my gosh! Do I actually miss Jake? School really does have me all turned around.

Rosa began telling Jake about her day as they entered the door to Ms. Fischer's classroom. The noise of the metal chairs clanging was barely audible over her voice. Both Jake and Rosa became even louder as they unloaded their days' events. It was the first time all day that they had a chance to talk with one another and in private.

Jake insisted Rosa should switch her last class from Visual Arts to Cryptozoology. "It's awesome! The teacher, Mr. Sylvia, is so laid back. He didn't care that I was late. I didn't even have to explain running across campus. Get this, we will be researching where Big Foot might live! Except for the class smelling like skunk, it's sooo cool!"

Ms. Fischer interrupted them, entering with her arms flailing. "QUIET! There is no talking when you are in detention, especially when you are in detention for talking! Keep your desks empty or you will have DOUBLE DETENTION if I catch you writing to one another."

What the heck is double detention?

After what was a rather busy day, spent figuring out where to be and at what time, Rosa rested her head on her arms as she fell asleep, watching other students hustling in the hall.

As Rosa began to wake, she realized no one was walking by anymore at all. "Ms. Fischer knows we have to catch the bus back to Robinson, right?"

The hour hand on the clock had done two full rotations. "It's almost five!"

For the first time, Rosa paid attention to how warm it was.

It's only January. How hot will it be in March. Hopefully, the school fixes the AC by that time.

Her desk had a sweaty imprint of her cheek and arms.

How could any Florida facility not have AC?

"Did she forget us?" Rosa questioned, as she looked towards Jake. Jake distracted in a world of his own was taken off guard, as if he also just woke up.

"Were you sleeping?" Rosa asked.

"No, I'm practicing visualization. You know that book that Mom got me. I think I have a new method to slip past Mike's guard the next time we roll."

"I thought I told you no talking!" Ms. Fischer said in a booming voice as she entered.

"Isn't detention only an hour?" Rosa asked.

"You're a sarcastic one!" Ms. Fischer responded.

"No, it's just that it is two hours now and well, the last bus?" Rosa asked as timid as a mouse.

"Fine! Go!" snarled the teacher. Jake and Rosa grabbed their book bags and ran toward the bus section of the parking lot, but no bus remained.

"We can walk, maybe jog a little. It's only four miles to Robinson." Jake said pulling up a GPS on his required school phone.

"We will miss dinner." Rosa said, looking over her shoulder at him.

"We run right past home. Mom will find something for us to eat." Jake said.

"NO! Mom can't know we screwed up on our first day! We are not stopping and don't you dare text her!" Rosa exclaimed, dropping her right arm letting her book bag hit the pavement.

Jake, confused, asked, "But why? She will under..."

At that moment, a shiny new black Lincoln Corsair pulled up circling and stopped right in front of them. The solid black-tinted driver side window lowered.

"Hey! Mike and Hunter mentioned you guys got nabbed by Ms. Fischer. Do you need a ride?" asked Abbey.

Rosa agreed, but Jake having already planned their walk, said his politest voice, "No thank you!"

He turned to Rosa, "Hunter is the enemy!"

Rosa shrugged her shoulders saying, "Mike's our friend," as she ran around the vehicle and climbed into shotgun. Jake tossed his book bag in first, took one last look and climbed into the back.

We aren't supposed to get in strangers' cars, but Mom would be even madder if I let Rosa go alone!

Abbey struck up conversation with Rosa. "So, the skinny on Ms. Fischer is she is blind as a bat. She compensates by ensuring no one is disruptive in her class. To her, 'disruptive' means making any noise whatsoever, even if it is answering a question she asked.

"When Hunter volunteered his answer of 'I did' it was his way of distracting Ms. Fischer. That is why Mike followed him with an 'I did.' It is guaranteed that if three students from different areas of the classroom say 'I did' no one gets detention. Jake, Hunter was trying to be friends!

"Oh, another thing with Ms. Fischer, if you do get stuck in detention make noise initially so she knows you showed up, but sneak out after fifteen minutes. That old bat can't see the clock so she will leave you there to five if you don't."

Rosa asked, "Hunter was trying to be nice?"

"Yes, he was." Abbey answered as they pulled into the Robinson parking lot.

Jake climbed out too fast for her to even hear his thank you.

We know Abbey. Mom would have been fine with this had she known; I think?

Abbey handed Rosa two bags. "In case you missed cafeteria hours." Abbey drove off.

"JAKE!" Rosa grasped his arm with her free hand to emphasize major importance.

"These bags are from Outback Steakhouse! Let's eat before we go in," Rosa insisted.

They walked across a road called Mango Avenue, which ran right in front of the school. The other side had basketball courts, a community pool, and a recreation center. They encompassed only a small corner of The Bobby Hicks park, which included a large freshwater lake with piers.

"I bet this lake has gators" Rosa commented.

Jake asked, "How did Abbey know what time we would be there?"

"Oh Jake, stop worrying!" Rosa answered, "She was probably on her way back home after picking up Mike and Hunter from school to sneak away for dinner. Do you know the Outback on Henderson Boulevard is the original? It started the whole franchise."

Dinner was delicious, Jake admitted, while he finished eating even the skin on his loaded baked potato. Rosa in contrast, saved most of her steak for Ted, but devoured the potato and steamed vegetables.

Upon entering the auditorium Rosa could see their duffel bags had been rummaged through. It was impossible to hide since, their clothes barely fit in the duffel bags the first time they packed.

Ted said, "I was on the first bus back, eager to get back in AC. Apparently, most of the bags got rummaged through. Willard megaphoned already that we shouldn't focus on it. That it was most likely some of the Robinson students looking for a prank, and 'we should be flattered they are acknowledging us at all.'

"The teachers don't care since so far no one is reporting anything of value missing. Do you know the sophomores and juniors are staying in the auditorium at The Academy of Holy Names on Bayshore, and the seniors don't have to overnight at all? Guess that is how they are fitting us all in here. I can't wait to grow up."

"Ted, you already changed into pajamas?" Rosa asked handing him her steak.

"Showered already, too. One of the apartments my mom and I rented in Miami was supposed to be next level self-sustaining energy efficiency. It had some really cool things to it, like a garden on the roof, but if you weren't first to shower during peak times you were not getting warm water."

Jake looked at Ted, "You're brilliant!"

"You only realized that now?" Ted responded, kidding.

Jake continued, "I was trying to figure out how we could sneak out early to practice Jiu Jitsu. We can do it by showering and changing early."

"Don't forget brushing," Ted glared.

Rosa smiled, "That works for me," although her motivation was to avoid showering and changing in front of the other girls.

The twins grabbed for their pajamas, but Rosa couldn't find her top. "Why would anyone steal my old pajama top?" she wondered out loud.

"Probably because it was rainbow striped," Ted said handing her an extra t-shirt he had.

Jake focused on observing the routine.

Three hours in the morning to change by alphabetical order, and three hours at night.

Cafeteria hours are from 7:00 a.m. to 9:00 a.m. in the morning and 4:00 p.m. to 6:00 p.m. in the evening. At 6:00 p.m. to 8:00 p.m. teachers and administrators walk around ensuring all the students have the mandatory school application downloaded on their phones. They are to receive lessons on how to use it today and tomorrow.

Willard walked by the exit doors next to their beds almost at even half-hour intervals.

But what about next week?

Jake askcd politely on Willard's pass about an agenda to next week 6:00 p.m. to 8:00 p.m.

"My name's not Willard, you homeschooled freak! It's TOMMY!"

Ted, Rosa and half a dozen other children began laughing.

"Jake it isn't you we are laughing at. It's Willard," whispered a kid in the bed near Jake's feet.

Rosa asked, "Jake, why do you even care?"

"Part of mission Carpe Noctem," Jake said.

Sensing the audience around her Rosa teased, "Jake you are a dork."

"The hallways are clear. No rotation schedule out there, from Willard or anyone else. So far so good for Carpe Noctem" reported Ted as he sat back down on the squeaky bed.

Rosa looked over. "Ted, you too?"

"It's our mission Rosa. You said you wanted in last night. Are you chickening out?"

"No. It's just, why are you calling it a mission?" Rosa said, perplexed.

"Rosa, EVERYTHING is a mission!" They answered in unison.

Well, if Ted was saying it then it must be cool enough not to get them picked on.

"Hey Jake, let's not let Mom know we got detention on our first day," Rosa whispered, worrying after lights were turned down.

Ted smiled, "Is that where you two were?" Laughing, he said, "That's 'back of the bus cool.' You two are going to fit in fine. Detention on your first day. I'm proud!"

Rosa leaning down from the top bunk dangerously close to making it tip, looking across towards Ted said, "I'm serious Ted. GTM doesn't find out. I gave you my steak!"

"Okay, I promise not to say anything," Ted said, happy.

His smile faded on the third CLICK CLICK, click click though.

Jake better be right on keeping these beds as part of mission Carpe Noctem because I'm starting to hear CLICK CLICK, click click worse than the thumping in Edgar Allen Poe's "Tell-Tale Heart."

EPILOGUE

Jake's chest heaved. A fishy scent tickled his nose. Smells don't tickle, but whiskers? Opening his eyes inches in front of his face— bright amber eyes adorned with flecks of gold—gazed back. They were astonishing and stood out even more as he noticed they were surrounded by black velvet. Jake stared. Warmth enveloped him. An overwhelming content embraced him. The panther purred.

Water splashed Jake from both sides. He glanced, reacting. The panther vanished. He was alone again. Alone in a gymnasium full of a thousand other students.

Everything was new to Jake and Rosa that day. It was their second night away from their family, their second night housed in a strange place. Jake tried to stay awake to ensure he was diligent observing everything possible for Carpe Noctem. A shared mission tying him to Ted and Rosa. They will prevail. They must. What other choice did they have?

The late evening hit an hour where observing was pointless. Any movement or observations after that time would be irregular and of no use in planning for Carpe Noctem. Hearing a slow rhythmic breathing from Ted's bunk below him, Jake drifted asleep around midnight. It was only due to his odd dream that he woke at the strange hour of 1:00 a.m.

The hallway doors click-clicked.

People using the bathroom most likely.

Jake heard Ted's breathing stagger then slowly return to a rhythm.

What an odd dream. I wonder if it means something. What a beautiful creature!

Focusing on his own breathing, Jake drifted back to sleep again. Jake's blanket, that covered his legs and arms, tightened. Half asleep, he tossed and struggled to sit-up, but the blanket—pulled tight from both sides—didn't give. Right as he became alert enough to yell a pillow silenced him. He couldn't see, could barely breathe and only heard muffled laughter, girl's laughter. Hits to his legs came next.

"Hey!" Nikki yelled as she pushed the girl nearest her. The girl let her grasp of the blanket go and clumsily fell to the floor.

The other side of the blanket gave way. The girl pulling hard on that side fell forward taking the blanket with her, half landing on Ted's leg awakening him. Ted hurried to his feet opposite her. Unknowingly, placing himself in between Nikki and the girl she shoved.

Jake's hands—becoming released—grabbed the pillow pulling the assailant suffocating him forward.

"Ow, my arm!" a pretty Asian girl gasped. She hopped to the floor clenching her elbow and stood next to the girl who initially woke Ted.

"Oops, wrong bunk!" a fourth blonde girl said stepping out from the foot of the boy's bunk, "Or was it?" She held out her left hand to help her friend on the floor up. "No worries, I have plenty on video already. Hunter's going to love this!" she said flashing a fancy cell phone in her right hand.

"Lily, what the hell is wrong with you?" Nikki demanded, as she stepped out from behind Ted confronting the blonde.

"Oh look, if it isn't 'Ants in Her Pants.' Don't worry, I won't leave you out this time! Wouldn't want your mom calling mine and forcing us to hang out together, again," Lily proclaimed as she turned what appeared to be an ant farm upside down on Nikki's bed.

The four girls chuckled as the dirt fell through the open lid of the ant farm. Lily was shaking it, flying ants and sand everywhere.

"Sorry, not sorry!" Lily said as she made certain to give it an extra shake and drop the empty farm container on Nikki's pillow.

"Oh, and if you must know, we were coming over here for you 'Miss. Ants in Your Pants,' but gifts kept on coming when we noticed you slept next to the homeschooled freaks!"

The group giggled. They left going back towards the other end of the gymnasium.

"Are you okay?" Nikki asked concerning herself with Jake and ignoring her ant-covered bed.

"Who are they?" Jake asked as he bent, touching the bruises on his legs.

"I'm sorry Jake. That's Lily and her friends. Call them the cool girls, the popular girls, the rich girls, whatever. Lily and I used to be friends until... well it's a long story, but we're not anymore. Her choice. Lily has had a crush on Hunter since elementary. She most likely thinks the video will impress him or something. She's always targeting me. I should've warned you when you picked the bunks next to me."

"Here's what they hit you with!" Ted said, holding out a sock with a bar of soap in it.

"You're fine. Toughen up! Hurt or not, you can't complain about girls hitting you," Ted said.

"I thought I was safe sleeping all the way over here away from almost everyone." Nikki turned away hiding her face.

"Hey, don't cry. Let's drag your pillow and stuff on your blanket out to the hallway and shove it in a garbage can before ants get everywhere," Ted said, grabbing the bottom corners.

"Jake, can you brush off any remaining ants for her while we go?"

Ted had Nikki wiping her eyes and smiling by the time they got back. Her smile grew wider as she looked to her perfectly made bed. There were creases in the corners of the sheets. It was also adorned with another blanket and pillow, Jake's blanket and pillow.

"Jake, thank you!"

"It's nothing. The sheets just needed a shake. Besides I'm not about to use a pillow or blanket again after that anyway." Jake sighed, then after a little hesitation, chuckled. "I would tell a joke about ants in a bed, but I haven't made it up yet!" His laughter grew. "I'm not going to lie, my bed is broken."

Nikki laughed also, "TBH, I thought I was the only kid our age that found puns funny. Those are hysterical!"

"No, no they're not! Don't dare encourage him, Nikki!" Ted said gruffly, before chuckling also.

"Wait, oh boy, I'm not laughing at the puns. I'm laughing at that! Now that's funny," Ted said pointing up toward Rosa.

Rosa—who slept through the entire ordeal—was unconsciously swatting at her own nose. Upon it scrambled a tiny ant frantically outrunning her hand.

"If we only had shaving cream," Ted said, smiling.

"It's like Gulliver's Travels when he's a giant..." Jake said.

Nikki finished his sentence, "...and instead of the island of Lilliput, it's the ant that Lily put on her nose."

Ted rolled his eyes. "This Man Mountain is going back to bed. Goodnight you two."

Just as everything settled, a megaphone blared and Willard yelled, "WHO STOLE MY ANT FARM!"

Nikki put a finger to her lips and gave a slight head shake, indicating to Ted and Jake the three shouldn't say anything.

Willard continued, his yell changing and becoming frantic, "I DON'T CARE WHO TOOK IT! THEY WERE MINE AND I WANT THEM BACK! THIS IS THEFT!"

Angering at being ignored, Willard started pulling sleeping kids blankets off them and kicked at lower bunk mattresses.

"STEALING! THEFT! DID YOU HEAR ME? I WILL HAVE WHO-EVER DID THIS ARRESTED. ARRESTED FOR LARCENY!"

The megaphone dropped down to Willard's waist. "They are my pets, my friends."

Ted rolled over, looking away from the defeated boy. Wait, Willard is upset over ants. He is helping a system which is forcing us to remain at school five full days a week. I remember how GTM said, 'They are stealing our children!' GTM must feel worse than Willard right now. She loves us and they took us, but how do you arrest a whole government on larceny?

Jake watched as two very large boys walked up and handed the empty ant farm to Willard.

Willard started to cry then yelled through the megaphone again. "I'LL FIND WHO DID THIS! I'LL FIGURE IT OUT! YOU CAN'T JUST TAKE THINGS PEOPLE CARE ABOUT! WHEN I DO, YOU'RE DONE! DO YOU HEAR ME? DONE!"

The two cronies followed Willard as he stormed out.

The next morning Rosa finally stirred. Ted and Nikki had gone off to the cafeteria already for breakfast. Jake who had been awake all night snarked, "Look who's finally awake. Did you sleep all cozy up there? Was it nice and quiet for you?"

Rosa glanced around before saying, "Jake, I was awake for the whole thing. The girl in the bunk below me jumped in before things got bad anyway or I would have. Did you really want me to do something getting you labeled with the stigma of being the boy who has to have his sister fight his battles? Now be smart, go get a new blanket and pillow before Willard suspects you. I told you I would have your back. It's what older sisters do!"

"Older by ninety seconds doesn't count."

"That's five times longer than that Coner McGregor fight you made us watch. Bet he doesn't whine about getting beat up by a bunch of girls!"

FOOTNOTES

1. ^ http://www.ushistory.org/libertybell/quotes.html
2. ^ Dictionary of American Negro Biography, s.v. "Douglass, Frederick."
3. ^https://www.dosomethin.org/us/facts/11-facts-about-literacy-america
4. ^ https://parks.ny.gov/historic-preservation/heritage-trails/revolutionary-war/default.aspx
5. ^https://modernfarmer.com/2013/11/old-time-farm-crime-embalmed-beef-scandal-1898/
6. ^ https://modernfarmer.com/2013/11/old-time-farm-crime-embalmed-beef-scandal-1898/
7. ^ https://www.jiujitsubrotherhood.com/starting-brazilian-jiu-jitsu/a-brief-history-of-jiu-jitsu/#Japanese?Jiu-Jitsu
8. ^ https://youtu.be/HMUDVMilTOU
9. ^ https://youtu.be/ZxgMGk9JPVA
10. ^ https://youtu.be/lvwzpxatTMg

Mary Mulligan was born the year the Vietnam War ended. Raised in a small middleclass suburb in New Jersey, she escaped the cold and now resides in Florida with her husband and four-legged fur-babies. After twenty-two years in the technology industry, earning a bachelors in Management Information Systems and, a masters in Computer Science, Mary made a change. One of her older special-needs fur-babies required full time attention so, she opted to author a book series which allowed her the freedom to spend as much time as desired with her dog.

The book series, Cadre Kids, is aimed to inspire young adults through fictional writing. A fun fact to the series is that most of the character names in the books are based on dog names Mary owned or has been acquainted with.

Please join Mary's monthly email list for fun updates at:

WWW.MARYMULLIGANBOOKS.COM

www.ingramcontent.com/pod-product-compliance
Lightning Source LLC
Chambersburg PA
CBHW071603110726
47908CB00007B/2218